FIRST MISSION

FIRST MISSION

DRAGON APPROVED™ BOOK FIVE

RAMY VANCE

MICHAEL ANDERLE

DISRUPTIVE IMAGINATION

Thanks to the JIT Readers

John Ashmore
Misty Roa
Kelly O'Donnell
Kathleen Fettig
Diane L. Smith
Deb Mader
Dorothy Lloyd
Jeff Eaton

If I've missed anyone, please let me know!

Editor
The Skyhunter Editing Team

Copyright © 2021 by Ramy Vance & Michael Anderle
Cover Art by Jake @ J Caleb Design
http://jcalebdesign.com / jcalebdesign@gmail.com
Cover copyright © LMBPN Publishing
A Michael Anderle Production

LMBPN Publishing
PMB 196, 2540 South Maryland Pkwy
Las Vegas, NV 89109

First US Edition, February 2020
Version 1.03, February 2021
eBook ISBN: 978-1-64202-751-8
Print ISBN: 978-1-64202-752-5

DEDICATION

To dragons... who knew you mythical beasts would give me so much. Here's to 100 more dragon stories!

—Ramy Vance

*To Family, Friends and
Those Who Love
to Read.
May We All Enjoy Grace
to Live the Life We Are
Called.*

— Michael

CHAPTER ONE

It was Alex's first weekend off since she became a dragonrider cadet. She was surprised the instructors cared enough to give any of them time off, although she was glad to have it. The events of the invasion of the Wasp's Nest were still hard to deal with.

Alex was spending her Saturday staying in bed far later than she could have gotten away with at home. However, she did wake up early enough to snag breakfast before the rest of the cadets made their way to the mess hall.

Hot chocolate and cereal were all the breakfast she needed. Currently, Alex had all of her blankets over her and was propped up on her pillow, casually flipping through her HUD to see what textbooks had been loaded onto it.

Underneath the covers, it was cozy. It was familiar, even if the bed wasn't hers, and she had no idea what the covers were made of. Something soft—that was the part that mattered.

Alex had found a book titled *Advanced Tactics for Dragon Battle Groups of Ten or Larger* and opened it. It was more than just trying to kill time; reading always kept her mind off things, and there was a lot Alex didn't want to think about at the moment.

From the looks of it, the entire curriculum had already been uploaded onto Alex's HUD. Every class's books were open for her to read whenever she had time. *Finding that out was a mistake,* Alex thought to herself, fully aware she was going to have to stay on top of her reading. It really was easier reading letters than Braille. She was glad she had learned in *Middang3ard* VR.

Ever since she was a kid, Alex couldn't pass up a book. It didn't matter what kind of book it was. She didn't care whether it was fiction or non-fiction, or if she liked the subject. If it was written and she could access it, she was going to read it like some kind of literature-craving hoarding-dragon.

Alex's love of reading had definitely benefited her with a wide range of knowledge. Some facts were useful. Others, a large number of them, seemed as if they were far too specific to be useful. But, Alex thought, better to know than not, just in case.

The dorm room door opened and Jollies flitted into the room, holding a plate of food far too large for her. She set it down on Alex's desk and then flew over to her own bed, which was across the room. "Still in bed, I see."

Alex pushed her HUD down so she could see Jollies. "Hey, it's been a long week," she argued. "You can't blame me for wanting to keep the day as simple as I can."

Jollies sighed as she threw her arms up in exasperation, her color changing from a soft yellow glow to deep blue. "That's exactly why we should be celebrating!" the pixie shouted. "We're alive! We need to capture our lives, and truly use them! We can't waste any time!"

Jollies zoomed around the room, doing a couple of laps before coming back to her chair and taking a seat. "I'm just saying, it's kinda lame to stay in bed all day. Unless you're hiding from something. I can't see you hiding from *anything*, not after what you did. Talk about badass."

Alex pulled her HUD back up and tried to ignore all the noise Jollies was making flying around the room and yelling. "I'm not hiding from anything," Alex muttered under her breath.

Jollies flew toward Alex's face, hovering below her nose. "Are you sure?" she inquired. "Are you telling me the whole truth or half a truth? Because I know something or some*one* you might want to hide from."

"What are you talking about, Jollies?"

"Two young men were asking about your whereabouts this morning. Both of them seemed very disappointed that you had decided to stay in bed all day. You sure you don't want to see them?"

And there it was, the thing Alex had spent her entire morning trying not to think about—Gill and Jim. Even when she had been running for her life, it had been hard not to stare at Gill's butt. It looked so good in his armor, and he was unbelievably smart and levelheaded.

Jim was a whole other problem, one Alex had never thought she was going to have. She had been crushing on Jim ever since they'd started playing together in *Middang3ard*, but she had assumed she was just never going to meet him. People from VR hardly ever met in person.

Yet, here he was. He was even hotter than his avatar. His jawline was laughably chiseled for a teenager, and he looked like he played sports. Beyond that, Alex felt like she knew him. He was the only person she had ever felt close to in VR.

Staying in bed would be so much easier than running into either of them, especially since she knew she wasn't going to talk to them. Yep, that was the best course of action.

Jollies poked Alex's nose. "Hey! Aren't you even going to ask me about it?"

Alex laughed as she tried to look Jollies in the eye. "No, I'm not since I don't care which boy was asking about me."

Jollies grasped her heart and mimed dying and falling out of the air. She lay crumpled on Alex's lap. "How could you not care?" she squeaked. "Two boys are madly in love with you, and you don't care who they are?"

"Nope. Not even a little bit."

"You're no fun," the pixie said as she walked down the length of Alex's leg. "Also, I noticed you haven't put your blindfold back on. And Manny's nowhere around. You're getting better at using your eyes, aren't you?"

"Yeah, a lot better. I'm not getting headaches anymore. Sometimes there's still too much detail, and my brain gets kinda wonky, and everything goes fuzzy. And I still don't know how to do any of the crazy stuff that dragons do with their eyes. But it's loads better."

Alex's HUD pinged, indicating she had received a message. Her heart skipped a beat as she realized it was probably her parents responding to her. "Hold on, Jollies, I think my parents just messaged me."

But it wasn't them.

Alex opened the message, and her heart sank—not because she was disappointed that it wasn't from her parents, but because it was from Jim.

The message read, **What are you up to today?**

Alex wasn't certain how to reply. On the one hand, she wanted to see Jim more than she had let on since Myrddin had suddenly introduced him from out of nowhere. On the other, Alex was terrified of sitting down and talking with him.

After taking much longer than she thought reasonable to respond, she texted, **Nothing much. How about u?**

Jim texted back. **Just going for a walk in the field after breakfast. Want to come with?**

Now Alex had to think.

A walk sounded nice.

It also sounded awful.

So much could go wrong. What if she said something stupid or blurted something that made Jim uncomfortable? Why was all this so hard?

Yeah, a walk sounds good.

Jim sent a smiley face and responded, **Cool. I'll see you at the field at a quarter past twelve**.

Alex's heart skipped a beat. Not only was he hot, smart, and capable, but he was also considerate about time, one of Alex's biggest pet peeves. This was definitely not a good idea.

Jollies looked at Alex, a grin on her face. "Why do you look so worried all of a sudden?"

Alex cast a disapproving look at Jollies. "What did you tell Jim?"

"Just that you would be spending all day in bed. And that you were dying for some company."

Alex instantly regretted having spoken to her roommate about how weird it was to see Jim again. She hadn't considered that the pixie was empathetic, and she'd completely forgotten what Jollies had said about pixies and their feelings.

Alex picked up her pillow and swatted at Jollies as the pixie shrieked with laughter and flew away. "I also told him you were madly in love with him." She cackled as she flew around Alex's head.

"Are you serious? Why would you do that?" Alex buried her head in her pillow and shook it. "That is not a cool thing to tell humans," she whined. "He probably thinks I'm out of my mind and wants to hang out to tell me not to be such a creep."

"Or maybe he's going to declare his undying love for you!"

Alex got off the bed and chased Jollies, who shrieked again. Her skin glowed bright pink as she zoomed around the room. "I'm going to kill you, Jollies," Alex shouted.

Jollies easily evaded Alex. She was just too fast. "I'm kidding, I'm kidding," Jollies said after she stopped zipping around. "I might be a pixie, but I'm not tone-deaf. I wasn't trying to make things *more* complicated for you. Just a little complicated."

"Well, you succeeded."

"When are you guys supposed to hang out?"

Alex looked at her dragon anchor to see the time. "In a few hours," she said. "And you and I are not on speaking terms right now."

Jollies flew to Alex's face and kissed her on the nose. "Hardly," she said. "We're on even better speaking terms. I want all the juice on this kid, and when you get back, you're telling me everything."

Alex sighed as she collapsed onto her bed. "All right, fine. But you have to promise not to be weird."

"Promise on my first set of wings," Jollies agreed as she held her hand behind her back, her fingers crossed.

Alex walked out onto the field. It was a beautiful day. The sky hardly had any clouds in it, and the sun was beaming down. It wasn't too cool or too warm. This was the kind of day to be outdoors. She wondered if she could take Chine out, or if there was some kind of paperwork that needed to be filled out first.

The time Chine and Alex had spent together so far had been training-related, except the battle they had narrowly won. It couldn't be weird for Chine and Alex to hang out, though. They were bound together, after all.

Jim was sitting under a tree in the part of the field where it met the forest. Alex wondered if the forest was also part of the Nest. She hadn't seen it before except from dragonback.

Alex waved at him as she approached, and Jim stood up to greet her. "Hey, Jaws," she said, trying to sound as casual as possible. Jim extended his hand to her. "Nice to meet you in person. I don't think we've been formally introduced." He smiled shyly as Alex took his hand, and they shook.

"Yeah, I didn't really get a chance to talk to you when you first showed up."

Jim pointed to the forest. "I wanted to check this out. I haven't seen a proper forest before, being a city boy and all that."

"Sure, and I'm pretty certain everyone playing VR games is a city person. Would you be playing video games if you had anything interesting around?"

Alex and Jim left the field behind. The forest was ominously dark, the trees growing thickly everywhere except on the walking path. "I highly doubt it. One of my favorite parts about VR was how much nature was everywhere. Even in the village."

"Do you remember that one elf village we went to? The one in the trees? That was wild."

Jim stared up at the canopy, nodding. "Yeah, that was pretty crazy. I wonder if real elf cities are like that. It would be amazing to see them. You know, in real life. I would never have thought they were real."

"Yeah, and what about the dragons?"

Jim turned to Alex, grinning. "Wouldn't have ever thought those were real either," he agreed. "I still haven't met a dragon, but then again, I'm not a rider, not like you. I'm part of the mech program under Roy. My dragon is metal."

"So, I'm still the only human rider," Alex muttered to herself.

"Excuse me?"

"Ahh, sorry. It's just that when Myrddin recruited me, he said I was the first human rider. Then you showed up, and I was kind of like, guess that didn't last long. But you're in the mech program, and, well, I wonder what's up with that?"

"Yeah, I hear that. I asked to be a rider, but I was turned down flat. Something about reaction times and not having a magical nature."

Alex sighed. "Too bad. You are an incredible rider."

"VR rider," Jim countered.

"Rider," Alex corrected. An awkward silence fell between them, and suddenly Alex just wanted to run. That wasn't an option, so she took another tack. "How did you get into the program? Did you beat the raid?"

Jim laughed and shook his head. "No, I failed every time after you got in. I couldn't even get into the bee vortex without you. No one would even listen to me when I told them how to get past the bees. Now I see why you didn't bother explaining and just did it."

"Yeah, sometimes people aren't going to listen to you. But you didn't tell me how you got in, you just told me how you didn't."

"Oh, yeah, that. Well, my dad is in the military, some really upper-level stuff. He's not even allowed to talk to us about it. But I figured, why not ask? If the VR game was a recruitment tool like everyone was saying, it would make sense that the military knew about it."

"Yeah, it would."

"So, I asked my dad, and he didn't want to tell me anything, but I kept after him. I showed him the game, all my stats and everything. He didn't say anything at first, but the next day there was this military guy in the living room. He asked me all sorts of weird questions, and then out of nowhere, he handed me an application."

Alex almost didn't believe what she was hearing. "Wait, you got into the program just by applying?" she asked.

"Not quite. Turns out, my dad has been working for the mech department of the dragonriders, doing a lot of organization. He told me that when I showed him my stats, he couldn't in good conscience fail to pass my information along."

"He didn't have a problem with his son going to war? He *did* know that it's a for-real war, right?"

"Of course, he did. He works for the military, remember? We had a long talk about it. He said it was my decision to make, and he knew I'd find a way eventually if I wanted. So, I filled out the application, and he got it to the right people."

Alex stared at the shadows moving throughout the trees. "That's pretty cool," she finally said. "I had to fight my mom and dad. They didn't let me go until I showed them what the VR world was like. I think they kinda forgot about the whole 'fighting the Dark One' part after that."

"Or maybe they thought you could handle yourself. That's what my dad told me. And most of the trust he has in me is because of you."

Alex looked away from the trees and met Jim's eyes. "What do you mean?"

Jim sat down on a tree stump and sighed as he clasped his hands together. "You're amazing on a dragon," he explained. "From the first time I saw you, I knew you were special. I always watched you closely. A lot of what I do when I'm in the air is because I saw you do it."

Alex blushed and turned to hide her face. As she turned, she saw Gill and Brath walking through the forest along the same path, heading right toward them. *Damn it,* Alex thought.

Gill waved amicably at Alex and Jim. "Greetings," he called. "It's a beautiful day, isn't it?"

Jim rose and reached out to shake Gill's hand, who took it heartily. "I've heard a lot about you from the instructors. You and Alex handled yourselves pretty well when the orcs came through."

Gill nodded, his face betraying no expression. "Thank you. Alex was invaluable to our defense. I've heard good things about you as well, Jaws, is it?"

"That's my call name, but yeah, Jaws."

"Myrddin seems particularly excited to have you riding with us. I hope you're a good fit for us cadets."

Jim smiled widely. Alex'd had no idea Gill could be so friendly. It made her wonder why he had seemed so cold to her.

"What are you guys doing out here?" Jim asked.

Gill pointed down the path. "There's a spot up ahead where I like to meditate. I was going to try to teach Brath how to calm his spirit and see deeper into his center."

Jim got down on one knee so he could be face-to-face with Brath. "I don't think I've met you yet either. My name's Jim, but my friends call me Jaws."

Brath slapped away Jim's hand and spat on the ground. "Three things. One, don't ever kneel to look a gnome in the eye. It's rude. We know we're shorter than you. Two, we aren't friends, human. I can hardly tolerate your kind. Three, you keep trying that nice human crap, I'm going to knock that smile off your face, you got me?"

Jim stood up, looking like he had just bitten into a lemon. "Okay, I guess. Nice to meet you, too," he muttered.

Brath pushed past Jim and walked past Alex, stopping for a moment. "Good to see you too, Boundless. Hope you two had a good walk, but a word of advice. You two probably shouldn't mate. You would have hideous children. I'm talking goblin-ugly."

Gill shook his head as he walked after Brath. "I don't believe in apologizing for friends, but I think we can all see that Brath might benefit from meditating. It was nice running into you two. See you around."

Gill and Brath disappeared into the forest, leaving Alex and Jim standing in awkward silence. There was a lot for Alex to take in. The easiest one was Brath's change of attitude to her. He didn't seem friendly in the least, but he did seem like he respected her. She could say the same about him.

Next was Gill. He was so cordial and outgoing to Jim. Did he suspect something? Was there a reason for him to, or had he just started to come out of his shell a little bit? Alex didn't know anything about drow or their personalities, and she did very much want to get to know Gill.

Which brought her to the next point, rounding out the topics she could obsess over for the next few days—Jim. Not the baby part. She couldn't care less what their kids would look like. She was more concerned with what their faces would look like if they were mashed together.

Jim cleared his throat as he awkwardly kicked a rock next to him. "What're you thinking about?" he asked.

"Huh? Oh, nothing. Nothing. Just lunch. Getting kinda hungry, right? I think I'm going to head back. All this exercise has got me *famished*. I'll catch you around."

Alex headed back toward the Nest as fast as she could, only realizing later how rude she must have seemed, running away from Jim after he'd asked her to go on a walk. It didn't matter, though. She knew things were going to get weirder soon enough. Might as well be the one to get it started.

CHAPTER TWO

Alex was making her way back to her dorm room through the Nest when she felt something tugging on the back of her mind. It was like having a word on the tip of your tongue; you knew it was there, but you didn't know why or how.

She had a rough idea of what that feeling was. She had felt it a couple of times since she'd arrived at the Nest. It wasn't something she usually had time to focus on, but it had continued happening. It was similar to how she felt when she was close to Chine.

Alex decided she would go to her room later. She would head to the stables now instead.

It didn't take long for Alex to find the stables, even with the Nest's halls constantly shifting and changing. Sometimes Alex wondered if the Nest was trying to make her life easier or harder. She still hadn't gotten lost, so maybe it didn't matter.

Alex stood before the entrance to the stables. She held out her hand, and the crystals provided her with the datapad. She pressed her hand to it and the doors split open, revealing the stables.

The lights instantly came on when Alex stepped into the room. This was the first time she had been in there by herself. Obviously, it wasn't a big deal since her credentials had worked without a problem. Alex made a mental note to start stopping by here more often. When everyone was gone, the stables were pretty calming.

Alex walked up and down the rows of dragon-outfitting stations. From what she had seen the last time she was here, the dragons used the areas above their stations as beds. The ceiling of the stables opened to the sky, so the dragons could come and go as they pleased.

There weren't any signs on the outfitting stations saying which dragon used which one. Maybe they were all inter-changeable, or maybe the dragons didn't need to be told what to do.

Alex reached out to Chine with her mind. *Hey, Chine, are you in here?*

The response hit Alex like a truck. This was probably the first time that she heard Chine alone before. Usually, they were surrounded by others. That probably did something to dampen the effect of Chine's psychic abilities.

You heard me calling!

Yeah, I heard you from halfway across the Nest.

I do have a loud voice, but I wanted to speak to you. Continue on your path and you will find me.

Alex did as she was instructed and followed the winding path until she came to a station she *knew* Chine was in. His tail curled around him and his wings relaxed, Chine was lying on what looked like a bed of leaves and flowers.

Chine looked at Alex, his eyes sharp and bright. *You should come up here.*

Alex didn't need to be asked twice. She climbed onto the platform and stood near the wall, uncertain of how close she should get to the dragon. Even though she had ridden Chine a handful of times, this felt very different. *What did you want to talk to me about?*

Chine rolled over lazily and huffed out a column of smoke from his nostrils. *There wasn't anything I wanted to talk to you about. I just wanted to talk to you.*

Oh, that's different.

How so? Do humans always have to have a reason to talk to each other? A pressing subject on their mind?

Alex shrugged as she stepped farther into the dragon's sleeping area.

Not really. But usually, when someone says they want to talk, it's about something specific. A problem or something.

Ah. I can drum up a problem if you want. I can be quite critical.

Alex raised her hands and shook her head.

No, no, no. You don't have to do that. We can just talk.

Come here and sit with me.

Chine lifted one of his wings, and Alex could see there was a nice spot to sit directly beneath it. She gingerly made her way over to her dragon, suddenly aware of how large and deadly he was, and sat beside him. Chine relaxed his wing, and it covered Alex the way a friend might put their arm over your shoulder.

Chine's wings didn't feel as leathery as they looked. They were covered in small scales. The dragon was very warm, and Alex felt like she was under a blanket.

Is this what you do all day?

Chine looked at Alex, his eyes sharp. Alex wasn't sure how to read them yet.

Not usually. The rest of the dragons are out at the moment. I thought it would be nice to have some time to myself, away from them.

I was going to stay in bed all day, too.

Alex, you don't seem very comfortable right now. Why is that?

Alex looked down at her hands, which she had clasped, unknowingly cracking her knuckles in turn.

How did you know?

We are bound together. There are many things we will know about each other, but I don't need to be a psychic to see you fidgeting.

It's not that I'm uncomfortable. It's just...I don't know; this is all very different than in VR. It's not unnerving, it's...it's all new. And it makes me feel like I might be doing something wrong.

Chine leaned forward and gently rested his chin on the top of Alex's head.

It takes time to get comfortable with the binding, even more so for those who played VR. I believe your dragons in the game are silent. Mere steeds. Dumber than horses, correct?

Alex bashfully looked away, ashamed she had expected Chine to be like that. *Yeah, pretty much.*

It only makes sense you would feel confused by riding a talking, thinking creature you have a telepathic link with.

When you put it that way, I don't feel nearly as dumb.

Exactly, Dustling. You have high standards. Perhaps don't hold yourself to them so strictly.

Alex relaxed a little bit and leaned against Chine. She had assumed the relationship between her and her dragon was going to be like having a pet, not a mentor.

Not a mentor, said Chine, *an equal. We are one and the same.*

A plume of smoke shot out of Chine's nostrils as he sighed. He took a huge, heaving breath that threw Alex off balance as she leaned against him. She could feel his heart beating through his chest. It felt nice, and it felt like they were closer.

So, what do you do all day? Alex asked.

Chine sat up and looked at the dragons waltzing with the clouds in the sky.

I usually think. There is much to ponder in the universe, and I am still young, and without the knowledge of my kind. It leaves much to the imagination.

What do you mean, the knowledge of your kind?

We dragons were raised here, away from the rest of our species. We did not receive the ancestral stories and legends, or the wisdom of our parents. It is a painful loss and yet a beautiful gain, for we are almost like the first dragons. We are free of our past to become ourselves.

Chine stood and stretched his wings.

My wisdom and that of my brothers and sisters is ours alone and no one else's. There is pride in that.

Chine was still staring at the sky.

Do you want to go for a ride?

Alex's heart leaped in her chest. She still didn't know the proper way to approach Chine about riding, but the dragons must love flying on their own. Alex was fairly certain none of the dragons flying above them had any riders.

Sure, I would love to!

Then let us go.

Alex jumped onto Chine's back and linked her dragon anchor to the collar around his neck. They both glowed the same color, then Chine leaned back on his hind legs, flapped his wings, and soared into the air.

The wind cut Alex's face, and she raised her HUD visor to cut back some of the light coming off of the sun. This was why she was a dragonrider—for each and every moment like this.

Alex got back a little bit after dinner. She went straight to the mess hall to see what was left over. She had forgotten the hall was magical and food was always stocked, hot or cold, depending on what you wanted. There was no line, so she piled on whatever she wanted. She was feeling adventurous today. Her heart was still racing from the ride she had gone on with Chine.

The two of them had floated high above the clouds and just coasted. They didn't speak. They'd watched the dragons dance beneath them and the clouds move across the sky. She had no idea how long she was up there. The only reason they'd left was that Chine wanted to take a nap before they got fitted for new equipment.

Alex had completely forgotten about the fitting and the mission Myrddin had assigned the new dragonrider team, having been caught up in the prospect of a full weekend off. Now taking a weekend for themselves made sense. Myrddin was probably just letting them catch their breath before they shipped out.

The mission Myrddin had explained sounded simple enough—provide backup for the mech riders while they transported minerals to craft weapons out of. Alex assumed the mission would be anything but simple, though, since Myrddin had made coming to the Wasp's Nest sound simple.

If the mech riders weren't capable of performing this mission on their own and needed backup, that probably meant Myrddin was expecting problems. Or he could just be setting the new team Boundless up with an easy win, something to grow their egos and knowledge. Who threw a bunch of newbs into the deep end?

Alex heard noises where the line usually was. She leaned over to see what was making the sounds.

Brath was getting food and something to drink. He walked closer and stopped when he saw Alex. Then he came over and put his tray on the table next to her. "Hey," he grumbled.

Alex, surprised that Brath had sat beside her, replied, "Hey."

Suddenly Brath groaned loudly and slammed his hands on the table while he blushed bright red.

"All right, all right, you don't have to drag it out of me by giving me the silent treatment," he exclaimed. "I hate doing stuff like this, all right? Hate it. So, I'm only doing it because I mean it. I'm sorry."

"Wait, what?"

"I'm sorry for being such a turd about you not being able to see and throwing you on the spot and junk and making you feel terrible. Okay? Do you feel better now?"

Alex had to hold in the laugh threatening to break out and spoil the sincerity of Brath's apology. "Yes," she said quickly. "Much better. And I appreciate the apology."

"All right, great."

Brath started eating and didn't look up again. He sped through his meal. When he finished, he stood and said, "And Gill likes you. He's not going to tell you, but he does. So, don't be a dick to him and break his heart or anything, all right?"

Then Brath said something quickly in Gnomish, spun in a circle once, and bowed before sprinting out of the mess hall.

Alex was left confused and annoyed. *Why did he have to go and ruin a great moment by telling me about Gill?* she thought. *Ignorance is supposed to be bliss.*

Later in the evening, Alex was sitting on her bed, scrolling through a book titled *A List of Abnormal Uses for Dragon's Blood*. She thought the book was gruesome, but it had captured her attention.

Jollies opened the door and flew inside, then sat down at her desk and started writing.

Alex looked up from her book, trying not to make it obvious she was interested in what Jollies was doing. But the pixie was too small, and Alex couldn't see over her shoulder. "Hey, you didn't bring back any food this time?" she asked.

Jollies threw a glance over her shoulder and smiled at her roommate. "I ate in the Hall," she said. "I was too excited. A letter from my parents came today, and I wanted to write back before we leave. Just in case we don't have time, you know?"

Alex's heart twinged. She still hadn't heard back from her parents. She wasn't sure if they had received her message, or if they just hadn't bothered responding. Deep down, Alex knew there had to be a good reason for her parents not to have messaged back. It wasn't like some unspoken terrible thing had happened between the three of them.

If Alex was honest with herself, she would think her parents were probably just too overworked to have figured out the technological part of messaging her. She remembered when she'd overheard her folks trying to figure out how to use Skype. She had wished she was deaf that day.

Jollies picked up her letter, sealed it in an envelope, and flew out of the room. She came back in a couple of seconds and flew up to Alex's face. "I told them all about you and how you're such a great roommate, and really fun, and super brave, and really, really, hot, and how we're becoming best friends but you're kind of standoffish like you're afraid of getting hurt but still really sincere."

Alex was taken aback by the revelation, but she tried to roll with it. "Wait, you told them I'm hot?" Alex asked.

"Uh, yeah, obviously. It's an important piece of information."

"And all that other stuff? You know, like about me being standoffish. You think that is true?"

Jollies perched on Alex's shoulder and stretched her arms. "It could be, but I'm a pixie and you're a human, so there's some stuff lost in translation," she admitted. "Honestly, most everyone but fairies or pixies seem standoffish to me. At least you aren't as bad as the gnomes."

"Yeah, I hear you on that."

"Talking to Brath is like trying to get a wall to develop a personality, then teaching the wall how to talk. But that's a teenage gnome boy for you. You almost ready to get fitted?"

Alex got out of bed and flipped her HUD up. "Yeah, almost. I've been dreading this all day. Last time I got fitted, I almost attacked Primrose," Alex said, then fell silent.

Primrose's death had slipped Alex's mind. For a second, she had completely forgotten about all the casualties from just a few days before. So many had died. Primrose was the only one Alex had known personally and, even then, she had only known her for a short while.

It still hurt like hell to remember Primrose's beautiful face, half-smiling, looking so content, lying in that casket. That death was entirely down to the Dark One.

Jollies must have just remembered as well. Her glowing skin had faded to gray, almost black. When she looked up at Alex, there were tears pouring from her eyes. "Funny, it only takes a couple of days of not stressing out to forget," the pixie said with a hiccup.

Alex tipped up Jollies' chin and shook her head. "No, it's not that," she said. "They're still in our hearts. We've just been... remembering we're alive. Life isn't back to normal yet. This weekend has given us a little time to pretend things are okay."

Jollies squeezed Alex's finger and nodded. "Yeah, you're right," she agreed. "We should probably get going and get fitted, though. Whoever it is probably won't be nearly as sweet as Primrose was."

"That's true. I'm going to have to make sure I don't attack them."

Jollies and Alex went down to the dragonriders' tailoring department. It was not the same place Alex had originally gotten her cadet uniform. Apparently, they were completely different departments.

Alex was glad she had listened to Jollies' advice about leaving early. It took them both a long time to figure out where the department was. By the time they found the door, it seemed like they had been wandering around the Nest for the last two hours, although after checking her watch, Alex knew that wasn't the case.

Jollies placed her palm on the datapad that appeared in front of the two girls, and the doors to the department whooshed open. The room was bare of any decoration. There was no one there, either. The only feature was a glowing blue circle on the floor that was giving out an ominous humming sound. "Hello?" Alex called. "Is anyone here?"

A mechanical voice answered Alex. "Hello, Alex. I'm glad you made it to your fitting. Please step into the circle so I can adjust your credentials and armor to official dragonrider status."

"Er, who are you?"

"Why, I'm the tailor. I'm an AI program created by the Nest to facilitate your uniform requirements. Do you have any more questions before we begin?"

"Uh, yeah. Can Jollies go first?"

"Certainly."

Jollies' jaw dropped as Alex stepped behind her and pushed her forward toward the circle. "By the gods, are you serious? I just told my parents how brave and caring and understanding you are!"

Alex laughed as she pretended to force Jollies into the circle. "I still am all those things," she whispered to Jollies. "But I'm also prudent, and not sure I'm trusting enough to obey a disembodied voice just so I can get a new suit."

Alex stopped pushing Jollies once the pixie was close to the ring. "I'm just kidding, Jollies," Alex said reassuringly. "I'm going to go first."

Jollies was gripping her chest and panting loudly. "You had me fooled!"

Alex stepped into the blue circle. "Ready whenever you are," she said.

The tailor responded, "Commencing armor and credential upgrade."

A bright light shot from the ceiling, creating the illusion that Alex had been encased in a blue tube, and the color of her armor started to shift. Within seconds, it was the red of the official dragonriders' armor. Then the light died.

The tailor said, "You may step out of the circle now. Jollies, please step into the circle."

Alex jumped out of the circle and patted her roommate on the back. "Doesn't hurt," she said encouragingly. "Go for it."

Jollies slowly flew into the circle, grumbling under her breath as she eyed the ceiling suspiciously. The same blue light shot down, and Jollies' armor changed to red to match Alex's. Jollies flew out of the circle after the light vanished.

Alex walked back to the circle, uncertain of where she should address the voice. "Thank you!" she exclaimed. "Can you tell us about the upgrades we got?"

The tailor answered in its monotone voice, "Predominantly, your upgrades are to the way your suit interacts with your central nervous system. Your physical abilities have been augmented, and you are able to access more information and menus in your HUD. Thank you for stopping by."

Alex and Jollies made their way to the door. "Well, that was kinda weird," Alex said.

"'Kinda' isn't the right word. Come on, we gotta go to the stables next."

Finally, Alex thought. She was really looking forward to telling Chine about the upgrades and even more excited to see what he was getting.

───────

When Alex and Jollies arrived at the stables, Tribble was walking between the two dragons who were up on their outfitting pedestals, Chine and Amber. Chine smiled down at Alex when she walked into the stables, and Alex felt a warm glow wash over her.

Tribble walked up to Alex and Jollies and nodded gruffly. "All right, let's get you ready," she grumbled. "Hope you got some idea what you're picking."

Alex did a double-take that made Tribble grumble louder. "So, you didn't read the email we sent?" Tribble asked.

Alex shook her head and avoided Tribble's eyes. "No, I-I mean, we get hundreds of emails a day," Alex explained. "It's hard to keep track of which ones are important and which ones should go in the trash."

"You got me there," Tribble admitted. "If there's one thing I want Myrddin to fix around here, it's the communication. None of us like being flooded with emails about what's going to be on the lunch menu. Not important."

Alex walked farther into the stables, approaching the platform Chine was lying on. "So, what are we supposed to do?" she asked.

Tribble came after her and pointed to the console on the

platform Alex was standing on. "Your new dragonrider credentials give you access to the different weapons configurations you can use with your dragon. They were pretty basic before since you were just cadets."

Alex thought back to the armor and weapons Chine had worn the last few times she had ridden him. They did seem pretty basic, just lasers and rockets. Now that she thought about it, that tech paled in comparison with everything around her.

Chine sat up and yawned lazily. *Looking forward to seeing how you would like to engage in battle, Dustling. Choosing weapons is more than just how you want to blow something up. Certain weapons provide you with different tactical options.*

Alex turned to ask Jollies a question, but the pixie had raced off and was gibbering to Amber, who was fluttering her wings nearly as fast as Jollies was. They seemed to be a good energy match.

Instead, Alex turned her attention to the console in front of her. She activated it and looked through the menus and options. The sheer number of choices she saw was overwhelming. It was like looking at the most complex skill sheet of an RPG.

The menus were broken down by dragon body part. The first section was for the feet, and then it worked itself up to the claws, the shoulders, the chest, and ended with the anchor. The diagram of the dragon on the console placed the anchor on his neck. Alex assumed that must be the collar Chine wore.

Alex clicked on the feet and almost wanted to shut down the console. There were over ten thousand choices. This was either going to take forever, or she was going to mess something up. "Chine, there are way too many choices," she moaned.

Chine's laugh boomed through Alex's head. *Yes, there are.*

If it makes it any easier, you don't have to look through each one. The console is psychically linked to me, as I am to you. If you think of something, an idea, I can relay it to the console, and it will show you something similar.

Oh, okay. That sounds more manageable, I guess.

Alex closed her eyes and tried to think of something that would be useful on a dragon's hind legs. She didn't think it needed to be something offensive since she'd never seen a dragon fight with their hind feet. All she'd ever seen a dragon do was rear up on their hind legs.

That gave Alex an idea—maybe some kind of stabilization, something that would give her the edge and round out her fighting capabilities if she were on the ground instead of the air.

Alex looked down at the console. There were only two options now, and one of them stood out to Alex. It was an augment that distorted the gravitational field around the dragon's feet that could either increase or decrease. *Now, that's interesting,* Alex thought as she selected it.

Next was the hands. *I'm partial to clawing and tearing,* Chine offered, *If that helps.*

Alex closed her eyes and imagined Chine tearing through the side of a mountain. *Yeah, it sure does.*

When Alex checked the console, there were a handful of claw enhancements—energy claws, fire claws, and things like that. None of them looked particularly interesting. Alex scrolled to the end. The last one was a stasis field generator, but it could only be used three times a day.

Alex read more about the generator. The field could be used to freeze an enemy, or the dragon could extend the stasis field outward, creating a concussive blast. You could even combine the uses into a massive attack. *Done,* Alex said as she moved on.

Now it was time for the chest. *I'd prefer something that doesn't rattle,* Chine suggested. *I have a sensitive chest cavity.*

Alex tapped the console to look through chest augments. She closed her eyes and thought. The idea of Chine's chest getting hurt was horrifying. When she opened her eyes, there were several choices. She picked an augment that boosted Chine's defenses and allowed him to deploy an energy shield around his chest. *Any ideas for your shoulders?*

I believe missiles are redundant since I can breathe fire. Also, they're loud. Maybe something to help with stealth? I'm not the, hm, most subtle dragon.

I know just the thing.

Alex chose a pair of misters for each shoulder. When activated, they would cover the dragon and the area around him with heavy fog. It would be perfect for throwing off the enemy and taking them out fast. *All we've got left is the anchor. What exactly is that?*

The anchor is our tie to each other. The augment of the anchor will give us an ability we share. It can be used together or separately.

All right.

Alex scrolled through the different augments as she tried to imagine what she wanted to choose. She stopped as soon as she saw the augment titled, The Unwieldy Element. When she looked up the description, she had to stop herself from squealing.

The Unwieldy Element allowed the user to cover their body with a random elemental aura that increased all of their physical and mental properties. It also set their body on fire. Alex chose it mostly for the latter. *Can we try it?*

Chine laughed as he looked around the stables. *It might not be a good idea for me, but you can give it a try.*

Alex read through the instructions on how to activate the power through her dragon anchor. She made a fist and slammed it against her hand, and there was a crackle of lightning. Then her body burst into flames, lightning flickering off of her.

Across the room, Jollies, Amber, and Tribble looked up as the flames across Alex's body started to fade. "Oh, my God, that's the coolest thing I've ever done!" the rider squealed.

Chine stretched his front legs, and his scales rippled. *Then you've made the right decision. It should prove to be invaluable on this mission.*

As Alex and Chine talked to each other, the door of the stables opened. Myrddin and Manny came into the stables, the old wizard looking more grim than usual. "I'm afraid we're cutting your weekend short. We're moving up the delivery date."

CHAPTER THREE

Myrddin curtly explained the reasons for the change in plans to the two dragonriders. He seemed rushed, as if he had little time to spend explaining the situation thoroughly, and he left as soon as he finished giving them the bare bones of the information.

Alex, Jollies, Tribble, and the dragons were left to try to put together the pieces from what Myrddin had said. It didn't matter, though. They were shipping out at the end of the day, regardless of why. That was part of being in the military.

Manny stayed after Myrddin left, and Alex came up to him. She thought about giving him a hug, but it might be weird. Not emotionally or anything—she just wasn't sure how squishy his body was. "Good to see you again, Manny," Alex said with a wink, pointing at her eye. "See what I did there?"

Manny laughed good-naturedly, with none of the stress that Alex had heard in his voice over the last few days. "Yeah, yeah, I see," he said as his eye tentacles waved about.

"I wanted to thank you for all your help, Manny. I don't

think I could have come this far without you. And I want you to know I really appreciate everything. Uh, are you a hugger?"

Manny shook his head as he turned his mouth down in disgust. "Oh, gods, no," he exclaimed. "Sorry, it's nothing to do with you, but Beholders don't do physical affection. Most of us don't even do positivity. But I appreciate what you said. And you're welcome."

"I'm going to be doing this one on my own. Just me and my new eyes."

Manny smiled proudly as some of his eyes vibrated in their sockets. It reminded Alex of how she had once read rat eyes vibrate when they're comfortable. "That's great news. I wasn't looking forward to another ride. So, Myrddin's spell is working well?"

"Took a little getting used to, but these are my eyes now. Time to put them to the test."

"Well, that's good to hear. You four should probably just sit tight here. Gill, Brath, and Jim took care of their fittings earlier today. They should be here in a little bit to take off with the rest of you."

Alex looked around the stables, suddenly realizing something. "Wait, aren't Roy and Toppinir supposed to lead this? Don't they have their own teams as well?" she asked.

Manny's eyes stopped vibrating, and he looked worried. "Actually, those two are going separately from you five," Manny explained. "You're going to meet at the mines and move the minerals from there."

"Oh, okay. I guess that makes sense. Well, I guess I'll just kill time then. Thanks again, Manny."

"I'm proud of you, kid. You've come a long way from where you were when you got here."

Manny left the stables. Tribble made eye contact, did

something similar to smiling but more confusing, and followed the Beholder.

Alex paced the area near Chine's platform, waiting for the boys to show up. By the time she looked at her watch, it had already been ten minutes. "I'm going to go for a walk." She double-checked the coordinates to the mine. "All this waiting is driving me insane."

Jollies flew to Alex and took a seat on her shoulder. "I'll go with you. I am unbelievably bored right now."

Alex waved at Chine as she walked away. *See you in a little bit, big guy.*

The two dragonriders peeked at the different dragon roosts and admired the dragons sleeping or lazily lounging about. For a while, they watched the skies as dragons came and went, flying at ferocious speeds.

Alex turned a corner and stopped. She could hear something in the distance, voices that sounded familiar. Maybe it was Myrddin, and she could corner him to get a better explanation for their sudden departure. Alex was still a little sore about her weekend being over.

There was an office, and the door was open slightly. Alex snuck over to it and pushed it open a little more so she could see who was inside.

Roy and Toppinir were inside, sitting at a desk and talking to each other. A three-dimensional map was projected between the two of them, and Roy was pointing to something Alex couldn't quite make out.

Then the map changed.

Now the map depicted a giant orb. The orb was not stationary, though. It was flying toward the planet like an asteroid, and if it was an asteroid, it was one of those world-ending ones. The orb looked huge in comparison with its destination.

The map changed again, showing a region that looked

familiar to Alex for some reason. She tried to figure out where she had seen it before, then it clicked. There was only one place she could have seen it—*Middang3ard* VR. Those were her only visual memories.

Alex tried to remember where in the game the region was, but she was too focused on trying to hear what Roy and Toppinir were saying to concentrate on the memory.

Roy leaned forward and pointed to a region on the map. "At this moment, who knows what the impact is going to be?" he grumbled. "On top of that, we don't even know what's in the SOB. All of our intel sounds insane."

Toppinir sat down in his seat and drew on his pipe. "What do you mean by 'insane?'" he asked.

"We got word from the Mundanes earlier today. They said the sphere is some kind of ship, and it's filled with genetic experiments. First thing that came to my mind was a biological weapon. I wouldn't have thought the Dark One would stoop so low."

Toppinir tapped the ashes out of his pipe and repacked it. "True. Even humans have the decency to steer clear of biological warfare. It's an extremely barbaric tactic. It seems odd, though. The Dark One would seem to have too much pride to try something like that."

Alex tried to push the door open a little farther. The movement made it creak.

How does a crystal door do that? Alex asked herself as both Roy and Toppinir leaped to their feet.

Alex attempted to look as if she hadn't been spying, but there was no way to hide it. Roy stomped over to the door and slammed it in Alex's face. "Guess we weren't supposed to hear that," Alex murmured as she stood up and headed back toward Chine and Amber.

Jim, Gill, and Brath were waiting for them near their dragons. Their dragons' platforms had been grouped together. Brath looked up impatiently as Alex and Jollies approached. "Took you guys long enough," he complained.

Alex brushed off Brath's words. She was learning how to deal with his constantly sour disposition. It was starting to seem rather endearing if she was honest. "Shut up," she replied. "We've been here for like an hour, waiting for you guys."

Gill was already atop his dragon Timber, sitting with his legs crossed as if he were meditating. "Brath had to talk to his sister. We were waiting for him."

Brath shot Gill a dirty look. "I didn't *have* to talk to her! We were just talking."

"He was uncomfortable about our mission today."

"Are you serious, Gill? I wasn't afraid! I just like to touch base with her and see how she's doing."

Gill looked at Alex, smiling mischievously. Alex's heart melted the moment she saw his sharp white teeth. "So, are we ready to go?"

There were no instructors or veteran dragonriders in the room. "Shouldn't we wait? You know, for someone to send us off?"

Gill stood up, his dragon anchor glowing. "We don't have to," he explained. "All of us are dragonriders now. We aren't cadets. We're technically veterans, even if we haven't fulfilled a mission yet. We've been given our coordinates and an ETA. That's how it works."

Alex leaped onto Chine. She didn't need to be told twice. The itch to get into the sky was strong. She was interested in the mission as well. Guarding a mineral delivery seemed easy enough, and they might have some fun along the way.

The rest of the dragonriders mounted and held up their anchors. Alex pulled up her HUD and opened her map. The coordinates had been marked with a large green spot.

Jollies was already on top of Amber as well, the two of them fluttering around. "What's the plan?"

Alex pointed toward the sky. "It's pretty straightforward. We go to the coordinates and take care of the mission," she answered. "Let's get going." Alex linked her anchor to Chine and pulled back on it, and the dragon soared into the air.

The other dragonriders flew after Alex, trying to match her pace. Alex's dragon wasn't the fastest, but her bond with Chine was the strongest. He didn't fight Alex's control like most dragons instinctively did. She and her partner moved as one.

Finally, the rest of the riders caught up with them. Alex looked over her shoulder and shouted at Jim, who was turning his mech on. The metal dragon stood up like a real one, its armor gleaming. She had to admit he looked very badass on it.

Then Jim pushed the wrong button or pulled the wrong lever because the mech stumbled.

"Didn't you read your owner's manual?" Brath asked.

Jim pointed to the HUD external on his temple. He pressed down on it, trying to regain control.

Alex pressed her temple too. "Some of us were too busy kicking orc ass to be bothered with boring reading material," she said on the comm, defending Jim.

Jollies came up beside Alex and Chine. Amber, her dragon, was roughly the size of a puma. Even though she was small, the thing looked dangerous. "How long do you think it's going to take us to get there?"

Brath groaned loudly. Alex was glad the comm picked up everything until they were turned off. "Is this going to be like taking a kid on a trip? Always asking from the back of the car, 'Are we there yet?'"

Alex laughed as Jollies blushed brightly, her whole body turning red. "Haven't heard that variation before." Alex giggled as she pulled up her visor to glance at the map. "Looks like we'll be in the air for a couple of hours. Three, max. Most airtime we've gotten so far, right?"

Chine breathed out a plume of smoke. *Good. It'll help ease us into riding together. No doubt it will take the team some time to learn your formations and the best ways to ride with each other and so forth.*

Alex was tempted to speed up but thought better of it. *The only way I ride is fast,* she said.

Chine turned back to look at Alex. *"Confidently" might be a better way to put it. Fast sounds reckless. And childish.*

Alex was starting to get Chine's dry sense of humor. *All right, no worries, big guy,* she assured him. *Confidently. We're going to ride confidently.*

Jim had scooted up farther in the formation, and he was now at Alex's left side. He looked at her, and they both smiled. Brath called from the back of the formation, "Hey, so, are you guys making marriage plans yet?"

Jim didn't bother turning back but laughed and told Brath, "You wear big words well for such a cute little guy. Do you want to be our flower girl?"

Brath seized his beard and tugged it hard. "Wait until we're on the ground, and I'll show you some of my big words!" the gnome shouted.

As Team Boundless flew toward the mines, Alex relishing hearing the voices of her group, and for the first time, her friends. It was almost like being back in VR, but so much better. Better than she ever could have imagined.

This was going to be a good mission.

CHAPTER FOUR

Team Boundless arrived at the mines before dark, the sun hanging low in the sky, and the air still warm. They were still too high to see much of the mines or the village surrounding them. *There is a lot of hot air coming up from the mines,* Chine noted. *Too much.*

Alex looked down to where she assumed the mines were. She closed her eyes, focused her breathing, and then opened them, trying to zoom in like she knew dragons could do.

It worked, and Alex's vision became even clearer. Her eyesight had increased dramatically, and she could see the mines beneath her. Flames were shooting out of a tunnel built into a hill. Actually, there were multiple openings, and flames were shooting out of all of them. There were no other dragonriders or mech riders in sight.

Alex waved the rest of Team Boundless down as she flew toward the mines. "They're on fire!" she shouted.

Chine hit the ground hard and Alex jumped off to see if there was anyone around who could explain what was happening.

The miners had scattered. Some of them were still

running as explosion after explosion rocked the mines. Others were sitting in the field, nursing burns while mages cast healing spells on them.

A crotchety dwarf with an obstinate expression was running between the different groups of miners, barking orders. He grabbed one of the dwarf miners, shook him a few times, and then motioned for the miner to join the others, who were carrying buckets of water toward the flames.

Alex ran up to the dwarf and cleared her throat before awkwardly saluting him. "Uh, hi. We're the dragonriders who were sent to pick up minerals. What's going on here?"

The dwarf glared at Alex as he threw up his hands. "What the hell does it look like? My mines are on fire!" The dwarf waved Alex's hand away. "Name's Rocten. These here are my mines, and these here mines of mine are on fire. Great flippin' day, am I right? Them's your minerals, right? Well, they might be burning up in there too, along with my miners."

"Forget the minerals. There are people still in there? What can I do to help?"

Rocten surveyed the dragons and their riders. "Huh. They're too big to get in there, but they could deal with the fire from the outside. Fire's coming from the inside, though."

Gill stepped forward away from the rest of the riders. "I can help with that," he said. "Fire isn't a problem for me."

Rocten eyed Gill suspiciously. "Huh. Ain't seen one of your kind out of the Veil before," the dwarf growled. "Don't matter. If you're offering help, I'll take it."

Alex exclaimed, "I'm going too. My suit has an elemental buffer. We'll take care of it."

Rocten pointed to the northernmost entrance. "All right. That's where the fire started," he explained. "Whatever happened came from there."

Alex hoped her dragon anchor power was enough to

withstand the fires, but she was going to find out. *Chine, can you use your mister to help smother the fire at one of the entrances?*

Chine nodded as he lumbered toward the southern entrances to the mines. "And the rest of you, get creative! We need to keep this fire from spreading," Alex said before grabbing Gill and pulling him toward the entrance Rocten had indicated.

Jollies took off with Brath toward the miners carrying water. The pixie used an elemental amplifier as Furi dug into the ground around the river the water was being drawn from. She and Furi redirected the river toward the mine.

Alex and Gill ran into the tunnel. Alex slammed her fist into her palm, and flames burst over her body. She was right; it was enough to handle the heat. Gill, on the other hand, didn't look fazed by the flames.

The two fought past the entry, trying to find the source of the fire. Most of the mine's entryway had burned, and flames were shooting sporadically from somewhere deeper in the mine. "Something's generating the flames!" Gill shouted.

Alex leaned over a ladder leading farther into the mines. "What could be doing that? That's not how fires work."

"Could be a weapon. Or a monster. The Dark One's forces might have sabotaged it!"

Alex climbed down the ladder, Gill following her.

Outside, the dragonriders were still helping the miners combat the flames. Jim and his mech dragon Croy were drenching the mines with water from the river.

Inside the mine, Alex and Gill continued to go deeper into its depths. Suddenly, Alex motioned for the drow to stop. She pointed ahead, unsure if Gill's darkvision was good enough to discern what she saw. "Oh, I see it now," Gill murmured.

Backed into the corner was a creature no bigger than a cat but shaped like a bear cub. It was covered in bright red fur and had large black eyes. Its face was buried in its paws as it cried. With each hiccup and sob, a blast of fire shot from its body.

Alex knelt, as did Gill. "That would be enough to start a fire," she said. "The poor thing is probably just scared, with all the mining going on."

Alex began to crawl toward the creature when Gill placed his hand on her shoulder. "No, let me," he said, moving forward.

As Gill got closer, the creature looked up. It squealed as it tried to burrow into the wall behind it. Gill didn't freak out, though. He merely reached out so slowly Alex couldn't even tell he was moving. Whatever he was doing worked; the creature stopped trying to dig its way out, and it got its tears under control.

Gill scooped the little red ball of fur up. "Let's get going and see if the others put out their side of the fire."

Alex and Gill climbed the ladder while the red creature held onto Gill's shoulders, tugging lightly on the drow's hair. The dark elf was suddenly even more interesting to Alex.

It didn't take long for Alex and Gill to find Rocten. The rest of the dragonriders had extinguished the mines' fires and were sitting around looking very pleased with themselves.

Rocten took the creature from Gill and cradled it in his arms, which looked even stranger than Gill holding the creature. "Blast it," Rocten complained. "No one told us there were firebrights in there. I'm sorry, kids, but we're going to have to clear out the rest of them unless we want the same thing to happen again."

The rest of the dragonriders joined Alex and Gill. "No problem. You guys take your time. Just let us know when you're finished."

"All right," Rocten said as he walked toward the mines.

"I'll let the rest of the team know. Thanks again for the help. You guys saved a lot of lives today."

Alex watched the dwarf walk away and couldn't help feeling a little bit proud. She knew her parents would be happy this was the first thing she'd done as a dragonrider.

CHAPTER FIVE

The riders and their dragons sat on the hills near the mines, watching the workers clear out the creatures responsible for the fires. Alex thought it was kinda funny watching the rough, dirt-covered dwarves cooing to the fire creatures they carried like infants.

Chine explained to Alex that firebrights were easily frightened. Sending out flames was a defense mechanism since they were considered to be delicious prey by many creatures that lived in and around mines, thus the tenderness of the dwarves.

Jollies was flying back and forth, her equivalent of pacing, and talking rapidly to Amber. It was odd to watch the riders talking to their dragons. Most of the riders spoke out loud, but Alex could only hear Chine, not the other dragons. She and Gill were the only riders who communicated strictly telepathically with their dragons.

Alex could therefore only listen to one side of the conversation. Jollies was usually thinking out loud, like now, when she was complaining about being bored. Brath, on the other hand, often voiced his frustrations with those around him.

Alex stood and stretched and called Jollies over. When the pixie finally came, Alex motioned for her to take a seat in her palm. "You know, there's nothing wrong with taking a break."

Jollies sighed, her body shifting to light blue. "I know," she admitted. "I don't usually care about getting up and going, but I've been cooped up in the Nest for *so* long."

"How long were you guys training before I got here?"

Jollies screwed her face up as she tried to remember. "I think I've been training for two years as a cadet," she answered.

"Are you serious? *Two years?*"

Jollies smiled and nodded as she stood up and pranced around Alex's palm. "Yep! That's probably why Brath was so mad at you when you showed up. We've all been at the Nest for a while, much longer than you two humans. Jim wasn't even there for a day."

Alex tried to come up with something to say that didn't sound like she thought it was ridiculous how quickly she had moved up the ranks. She did think it was strange. "You know, it probably has to do with the VR program we were in," Alex suggested. "It was supposed to be like a recruitment thing, but probably it also doubled as training."

"That would make sense. Most of us didn't even think there were dragons when we applied for the program."

"Wait, you just applied too? That's how Jim got in."

Jollies leaped off Alex's hand and danced in the air for a second before letting herself fall. "Yeah, that's how all the other races get in. None of us had a VR game of *Middang3ard*, only the humans. I heard it's because none of us needed to be convinced there were other realms."

"Why's that?"

"We already knew about them. Humans are the only ones who lost touch with magic. We might be fantasy creatures to you, but to us, you're just humans—one of many races."

Gill walked over to Alex and took a seat beside her. "The anchor power you chose worked really well. You made a wise decision."

Alex wished she could hide under a rock, but she managed a smile instead. "Thanks," she muttered. "Are you immune to other elements, or is it just fire?"

"Generally, any elements found underground. That's where we drow are from originally. Intense heat, dark magic, necromancy, and things of that sort don't affect us."

"That's really cool. Also, you did a great job of calming down the firebright. I don't think I could have done that. Back on Earth, I was terrible with kids. They hated me."

Gill brushed the hair out of his eyes as he smiled sweetly. Alex's heart melted once again. It was a wonder it wasn't a permanent puddle by now. "I'm the oldest of six. Most of my life was spent minding children," Gill explained. "My mother said I exuded a calming air, more so than other drow. We have a bad reputation."

Alex looked at Rocten. "Yeah, I noticed the way he was talking to you," she admitted.

Gill laughed as he leaned back against the hill. "That's nothing. Wait until you see how other elves treat me."

"That sounds rough. But I can understand people treating you differently for reasons you can't control, like Brath."

Gill looked at the gnome and laughed. "Oh, him? He's a jerk to everyone. It doesn't matter if you're blind, strong, or handsome. Any defining feature is fodder for him. He's warming up to you, though, as he always does."

Alex thought back to the last time she and Brath had spoken and what he had told her about Gill. She wished the gnome had kept his big mouth shut. "Uh, I gotta go," Alex muttered as she walked toward the meadow behind the hills.

Jim noticed Alex was leaving, and he stood and called after her, "Hey, you mind if I tag along?"

Alex stopped dead in her tracks and let out a heavy sigh, one that felt as if she were exhaling every irritating thing in her life at the time. She hadn't joined the dragonriders to get wrapped up in some Victorian love triangle. "Sure, Jaws," she said without turning around.

Jim jogged to catch up with Alex. She didn't bother slowing her pace, though. If she could have, she would have started running and not turned back. She did turn around, however, and when she saw Jim's smiling face, she forgot about everything.

The two humans walked down through the meadow. It was spring, and the harrigolds were in full bloom, their twisting yellow petals casting themselves to the winds to be carried away. Jim walked up beside Alex. "So," Jim started. "I heard through the grapevine—"

Alex interrupted Jim, nearly shouting, "That I was blind!"

Jim practically jumped back from Alex's tone of voice. "Whoa, no, not like that. I mean, I wasn't trying to say it like that. It's just, I had no idea. You never mentioned it in—"

"Because I prefer not to be known as the blind girl. It gets pretty old."

Jim nodded as he thought about what Alex had said. "I would never think of you as 'the blind girl.'"

"Yet here you are, asking me about being the blind girl."

"No, here I am asking one of my close friends about what's going on in her life."

Alex stopped walking and glared at Jim. She had no idea why she was so angry at him right now, but she felt like she could have hit him. The anger faded and was replaced by embarrassment. "I'm sorry. It's just, the whole being blind thing has been a problem since I got here. It's been obnoxious."

Jim continued walking, and Alex kept pace with him. They walked over to an old tree stump that stuck up amongst the yellow harrigolds. "Yeah, I can imagine. I wouldn't want to be talking about that all the time. How have you been holding up?"

Alex leaned forward, picked one of the harrigolds, and shrugged. "No one in VR knew I was blind, and I tried to keep it that way. I don't like people treating me differently, or like I can't do things."

"Seems like no one here would treat you like that. What's it like for you now, suddenly being able to see?"

Alex thought about the best way to answer the question. It was hard enough to explain what being blind was like. Take that experience and add on seeing through the eyes of a Beholder for the first time, and after that, being granted the eyes of a dragon.

It was a bit much to explain. "I guess it's been," Alex started, "complicated. It's completely changed my life, not that I thought my life was lacking before. It's just an entirely new existence. The whole world is different than I've ever known."

Alex held up the harrigold she'd picked so the sunlight glowed through the flower's thin petals. "The only time I had ever *seen* before was in a place that wasn't real, or at least, not like the real place. I've never seen my parents with my own eyes. I've never seen anyone from my old life with my own eyes. It's…it's different."

Jim nodded as he listened. "What about me? You've seen me as an avatar and now real life. What's that like?"

Alex tucked the flower behind her ear and laughed. "You? Yeah, I saw you in VR, but seeing you in real life for the first time was, ah, interesting."

"Oh, yeah? What was interesting about it?"

You're freaking hot, Alex thought. Probably not the best

thing to say right now. "You looked pretty much like your avatar," Alex finally said. "I heard that wasn't something most people did. I'm not sure how much my avatar looks like me. You know, I couldn't really use a mirror."

Jim moved, so he was right in front of Alex, looking her in the eye. Alex wanted to turn away, but something kept her eyes glued to Jim's. "Hm," he said. "You don't look different. Guess you don't need to see yourself to know what you look like."

Jim didn't move and kept staring into Alex's eyes. Alex couldn't tell how long they looked at each other, but she didn't want to look away. She felt like she could spend the rest of the day with him like that.

Thankfully, Chine broke Alex's concentration. *He's thinking about asking you on a date.*

Alex maintained her look of stoicism, but her heart was racing. A date? She'd never been on a date. She'd never even thought about going on a date. Why would she want to do such a thing?

Chine interrupted Alex's train wreck of thoughts. *He's very nervous.*

Before Alex realized it, she had already opened her mouth and was saying, "Of course, I'll go on a date with you."

Jim's eyes widened as he stood up, awkwardly trying to shove his hands in his pockets, only to realize he didn't have any pockets. "What? I wasn't asking, I...wait, how did you know I was going to ask you?"

"Call it a hunch. After this mission. Lunch or coffee? I don't know what people do on dates."

"I think since I asked you, I'm supposed to come up with ideas."

"Technically, I think I just asked you, but sure, take the pressure off me."

Just then, a siren went off near the mines. Alex jumped to

her feet, looking in that direction. "Guess that means it's time for us to go."

CHAPTER SIX

By the time Alex and Jim got back, the rest of the dragonriders were ready to go. Four of the mech riders had arrived and loaded up the minerals. It was explained to Alex that the mech riders rode in prototype mechs based on dragon physiology. The mech tech hadn't worked out as originally planned, and these were really only good for transportation.

Roy was the only rider who had managed to "meld" with his mech, whatever that meant. Alex got the gist of what was being said, though. Since they didn't have proper reaction times, the mech riders were sitting ducks in the air, and Jim was one of them.

As well as the mech riders, six more dragonriders had arrived. They were veterans and didn't seem to have any time to waste talking to the newbies. Alex tried not to take it personally. The veterans probably thought Team Boundless would need babysitting.

One of the veteran riders, a wood elf named Alborn, stood atop his dragon, a beautiful purple lightning dragon with white horns curled like a ram's. "All right, Team Boundless, I'm glad you've finally decided to join us."

Alex ignored the irritation in Alborn's voice as she mounted Chine. "Seems like we were the ones who were waiting around for you to show up," she called back. "You missed the fire and everything. Or did you not bother to ask Rocten?"

Alborn's eyes narrowed as he frowned at Alex. "I see respect for seniority doesn't mean much to humans."

"No, not really. And last time I checked, dragonriders are equal across all boards, right? It's not like you outrank us, so you should probably stop talking to us like you do. Boundless? You guys ready to go?"

Team Boundless stared at Alex, dumbfounded. None of them had been expecting her to talk back to the veteran riders. Earlier, Brath and Jollies had been fawning over them.

Alex wasn't impressed by the veterans. It wasn't that she thought she was better than them; quite the opposite. As far as Alex was concerned, the only respect you should give to people was what they gave to you. Life was that simple.

There was a reason Alex was a dragonrider, and now wasn't the time to pretend she had gotten in by mistake. Manny, Myrddin, and her parents believed in her, and more importantly, she believed in herself. If Alborn wanted to talk trash, he could suck it.

Team Boundless was going to get the mission done. She didn't need to be on good terms with every dragonrider for that to happen.

Alex double-checked her coordinates, linked up with Chine, and took off for the skies. She hit her comm and patched into the mech riders. "You might want to head up with us," she suggested. "We need to make sure we have you guys surrounded in case something happens."

The rest of Team Boundless took to the air, along with

the mech riders. Alex moved to the front of the formation and said, "Guys, I think taking a five-point position will work best. One of us in the front, one on each side, and two in the back. That sound good?"

Brath moved toward the back, explaining, "Furi's a little rowdy. Might be better to be in a spot where he can stretch his wings if something happens."

Jim moved to the back too and said, "I think we can be of use back here."

Gill and Jollies went to the sides of the formation without saying a word. Alex took the front, and they headed toward the coordinates as the other dragonriders took off and tried to catch up with them.

Alex noticed the other riders were trying to reach them, and she slowed her pace so they could ride beside Boundless or join the formation. Alex turned to Alborn. "I think we got off to a bad start. Name's Alex. Glad to be working with you."

Alborn looked extremely taken aback by Alex's straightforwardness. Finally, he grinned and nodded. "Wasn't expecting such a strong-willed teenager," Alborn admitted. "Glad to see you know how to handle yourself, though."

"Ass or not, we have each other's backs. We have *your* back. The mission and the team will always come first and foremost."

Alborn rubbed the back of his neck as he chuckled. "Your level of professionalism is starting to make me look bad." He sighed. "But you're right. When we reviewed the coordinates earlier, it looked like we could shorten the travel time by cutting through the valleys to the east."

Alex brought up her map and looked at the valleys. "Hm...yeah, it looks like they cut straight through to where we're trying to go. Sounds good to me. You want to take point?"

Alborn nodded and motioned for his team to take the

foremost position in the formation, so Team Boundless was following them.

Chine's voice came through Alex's head. *That was mature of you.*

Alex shrugged as she stared at the clouds. *Eh, I don't think it was that mature.*

I highly doubt Brath would have done that.

Okay, if Brath is the standard, anything I do for the rest of my life will be mature.

Alex turned her attention to the skies as Team Boundless, the mech riders, and the rest of the dragonriders headed toward the valleys.

CHAPTER SEVEN

The dragonriders descended into a canyon. Its stone walls were white as alabaster, and the air was cooler than higher up in the sky. The valley was deeper than it looked on the map.

They flew farther into it. Alex imagined this was what the Grand Canyon would have looked like if she had ever seen it. The canyon was deeper than anything Alex had ever seen in *Middang3ard*.

It wasn't hard to be impressed. Alex had read about how such things were formed, thousands and thousands of years of water slowly eroding the stone and earth until something massive and awe-inspiring remained.

A rush of cold wind blew past her face, chilling her nose and making it run, so she had to wipe it. She couldn't wipe the smile off of her face, though.

Alex looked around at the faces of the other riders to see if she was the only one who was obviously having a good time. The members of Team Boundless were either smiling or grinning widely, even Brath. Alex was glad she was surrounded by people who loved to ride as much as she did.

Up ahead in the formation, Alborn pointed to the crags in the canyon's wall before hitting his comm and saying, "This is one of the oldest canyons in the realm. They say it's the realm's equivalent of your Grand Canyon."

She knew it! But then she thought about it and realized she wasn't sure what it was she knew. "What do you mean, 'the realm's equivalent?'" Alex asked.

"That's the way the realms work. You can think of them as sandwiched on top of each other. Granted, each realm has its own quirks, but some of the geographical placement is similar. Most of the realms have a variation of your Grand Canyon in or around the same place. This one is nowhere near as large as the one on the human realm, though."

Alex smiled as she looked around and tried to take the canyon in. She knew her parents would get a kick out of hearing that she had seen the Grand Canyon or something like it, despite not being on Earth. Alex felt a twinge of guilt, wishing she could share this with her parents.

At the same time, Alex was very glad this was hers alone —these people, this adventure, all of it. This was an experience she was never going to forget.

Jim's voice came through on Alex's comm. "Hey, you ever go to our Grand Canyon?"

Alex hit her comm to turn it on. "No, I never wanted to. My parents tried to take me once, but if the trip was to take in its wonders, I didn't see the point," Alex said, remembering how much her decision had upset her parents.

"Well, are you glad you're finally getting to see it now?"

Alex turned back and pointed toward the sky. "I heard the one we got back home is even bigger than this. Now I do want to see it."

Static crackled across Alex's comm and cut off her conversation with Jim. The static got louder and she turned it off, hoping that resetting it would get rid of the noise.

When she turned it back on, she heard Alborn's voice. "We might have a problem," he said. "Look down."

Alex leaned over so she could see past Chine's shoulder. It was hard to make out, but it looked like there were riders down at the bottom of the canyon. She squinted so she could see more clearly; there were definitely riders below. "So, what, there are people down there?" she asked.

"The canyon is strictly a no travel zone for civilians. There shouldn't be anyone down there, let alone that many. I'm counting at least thirty bodies. That's not good."

Brath's voice came through over the comm. "Who cares? They're down there, and we're up here. All we have to do is keep that up. We're way too high up to be fired at."

Chine interrupted Brath in Alex's head. *Alborn is right; this isn't good. And it is about to get much worse.*

At the bottom of the canyon, the riders, clothed in black and atop black steeds, rode on, the wind of their passage echoing up the canyon's walls. The feet of the steeds were not hooves. They were the talons of birds of prey.

At a sign from the rider at the head of the posse, the rest of the riders pulled off their clothes, revealing their identities. The riders were trolls.

Once the riders had tossed away their cloaks, the magic shielding their steeds disappeared, and they were revealed to be bizarre birdlike creatures. The foul creatures looked humanoid, although their bodies were elongated and contorted.

They were sinewy and covered in sparse gray feathers. Their necks stretched uncomfortably long, ending in vulture heads, the skin thin and rotten-looking. They each had four mangy wings. A golden cap was fitted on their beaks, open to show rows of sharp teeth.

Alborn pulled up on his dragon, preparing to send it back into the sky. "We got vrosks and trolls," he shouted.

Alex had never seen a vrosk, but she had seen trolls in *Middang3ard* VR. If these things were like those she was used to, they could be up to ten feet tall. She didn't want to think about how big the vrosks must be.

The rest of the dragonriders took their cues from Alborn and headed back up toward the sky, but it was too late. There were at least fifteen vrosks and trolls above them. It was an ambush, and they were hemmed in.

Alborn cursed under his breath and furrowed his brow, running through his options. Alex saw him thinking, very aware that if he didn't figure something out soon, the Dark One's forces were going to close on them like a pair of scissors. It wouldn't be hard for them to steal the minerals after that.

The vrosks above started to descend slowly, taking their time, likely relishing the fear they knew they were instilling in the dragonriders.

Alex hit her comm and called to Alborn, "Hey! I think I know what we should do!"

Alborn wiped away the sweat forming on his brow. "I didn't ask you what we should do! Hold on, I'm thinking!"

Alex knew there wasn't any time. The longer Alborn thought about what needed to be done, the worse position the dragonriders would be in. *Chine, you ready for this?* Alex asked as she looked at her dragon anchor.

The scales across Chine's back rose and fell. *Yes, Dustling. I am.*

Alex hit her comm, bringing up all channels. "Team Boundless. We are engaging the enemy beneath us," she commanded. "Mech riders, I want you down there too. Brath and Jaws, you split from the back and take the sides. Gill, I want you on top, shielding them."

Alex pointed to Jollies and Amber. "Jollies, you're with me. We're going to thin out the party beneath us. Dash in and out. Get at least half of them, and then we regroup up here. Then all of us will push up and scatter the forces above us. Then we bring the fight to the canyon."

Jim shouted, "Are you kidding me? You want to *engage*? They outmatch us—"

"Wasn't a suggestion, Jaws. Go!"

Alex didn't wait to see if anyone followed her. She tore straight for the vrosks and trolls beneath her, scanning through her inventory to see if she had any weapons stored. *Should have checked that before I left.* She laughed to herself.

CHAPTER EIGHT

Alex descended so fast it felt like the wind was slicing her face. She held out her dragon anchor, and a scythe appeared in her hand. The scythe was nearly the size of her body, and she was surprised she could lift it with ease. *Never used one of these before. Should be fun.*

Jollies flew at Alex's side, barely visible in her peripheral vision. If the pixie was here, that meant the rest of Boundless probably had come as well. Alex hadn't even thought about asking what anyone else thought they should do; she'd just acted. Hopefully, it had been the right decision.

The vrosks beneath Alex and Jollies still hadn't given any indication they had noticed Jollies and Alex heading toward them. *I was right,* she thought. *They were expecting us to go straight up and take on the vrosks overhead.*

Alex turned her thoughts toward Chine. *Hey, how do we use your augments? Do I need to tell you anything or activate the—*

Chine stretched his wings out, slowing a little as they prepared to attack. *Same as flying—we're connected as if we were one body.*

Alex smiled as her dragon anchor glowed. *Perfect.*

Chine hit the ground amidst the vrosks and trolls at full speed, tearing it up with his claws. He breathed a plume of ether fire into the air and his gravitational augments activated, increasing the gravitational pull on everything on the ground.

Now that gravity had been increased, the vrosks had ground to a stop, as had the trolls, all of them weighed down by a force of nearly a twenty gees.

Alex leaped off Chine, slamming her dragon anchor to her chest as she spun her scythe around her back before bringing it back to her dominant hand and slicing off the heads of three trolls in one sweeping move.

Behind her, Amber and Jollies flew forward, the pixie activating one of Amber's augments that caused the lightning sparking off the dragon's body to echo a shadow of her movements as she increased in speed, leaving behind afterimages of herself that vibrated with electricity.

Jollies flew between as many of the trolls as she could, ramming Amber into them, leaving an image of the dragon and shocking their bodies with electricity.

Alex spun around and sliced at a troll who was holding a rifle, cutting it down before it could fire.

Up at the top of the canyon, the vrosks were beginning their descent upon the remaining dragonriders and the mech riders. The vrosks swooped down as the trolls hurled energy-charged spears.

Gill raised his dragon anchor, and Timber deployed a forcefield that spread over the riders. The energy spears collided with the forcefield, exploding and sending sparks flying everywhere.

The vrosks pulled up, trying to avoid the sparks, but many of them were caught in them. Then Brath detached from his position and flew toward the vrosks as Furi shot fireballs. The veteran riders just looked around as if they were caught in their first battle.

On the ground, Jollies was getting ready to rejoin the rest of the riders. Alex had leaped back onto Chine, and they were headed up as well.

One of the vrosks reared its head, and its beak glowed an icy blue before it fired a volley of icicles at Jollies. They hit Amber and the pixie head-on, nearly knocking her from her dragon. They veered to the right and crashed into the canyon wall.

Alex turned Chine's head to face the vrosks again, and he shot ether fire at the vrosks. They scattered, giving the pair enough time to get back on track, and the two riders flew as hard as they could to meet the others.

Once Alex and Jollies were back with the other riders, she was able to assess the situation. The vrosks and trolls at the bottom of the canyon were still reeling from the attack. Now would be the best time to put an end to them, but doing that would require leaving the minerals with minimal defense again.

Alex glared at Alborn, waiting for him to get his head in the game. The elf still appeared confused by what was happening. "Are you going to do something?" Alex shouted at him.

The vrosks above swooped down on the dragonriders, showering them with ice as the trolls continued to pepper Gill's forcefield with spears. "It's gonna give any moment now!" the drow shouted.

Alex, fed up with waiting for Alborn, pointed to the canyon. "We all move down!" she shouted. "They still haven't recovered, and we aren't going up anytime soon. Mechs, you're coming with us! So are the rest of you!"

Alex's comm opened again to a hearty agreement from the mech riders. She and her dragon made the first move, plummeting toward the canyon floor. Alex knew her trick wasn't going to work twice. She still had the element of recklessness on her side, though.

Just before Chine collided with the ground, he pulled up, soaring over the vrosks. Alex figured if they couldn't take on all the vrosks and trolls, they could at least avoid their attacks. She hoped speed would win out, and they could make it to the drop-off point and get reinforcements.

As Alex and the rest of the riders passed the vrosks and trolls, the canyon walls began to shake.

The wall to Alex's right exploded in a hailstorm of rocks and gravel as a fiery hand pushed its way out, followed by a flaming skull with curled horns. Sulfur and soot filled the air as a balrog stepped from the stones, a flaming whip in each hand.

Alex collided with the canyon wall as Chine tried to straighten out. "You have got to be kidding me!" she shouted as the dragon reared, then turned around. "All right, Boundless, this is where we make our stand. Jollies and Gill, you take care of the vrosks above. The rest of you with me! Mech riders, you keep going. Make it to the rendezvous."

Jim and Brath flew up next to Alex, along with the remaining dragonriders of Alborn's party.

The vrosks from above had met up with the vrosks at the bottom of the canyon. The balrog stood before them all, cracking his whip as he roared in fury.

Alex's heart was in her throat. At her side, Jim turned and smiled weakly at her. "Guess this is where we die. Nice knowing you."

Alex shook her head and shouted, "We've been through worse than this, Jaws!"

"Yeah, in VR!"

"Just means we got permadeath now!"

With that, Alex and Chine charged forward. Alex

slammed her dragon anchor to her chest, and her and Chine's bodies were covered in an icy armor as the dragon raised his glowing right claw. A concussive force shot out like a cannon, knocking the balrog back.

It roared in rage as it cracked its whip, pushing the vrosks and trolls forward. The vrosks sped past Alex. It was obvious her and Chine's fight was with the balrog.

Gill was right behind Alex. Jaws and Croy were in the air, firing heat-seeking missiles. Alex breathed a sigh of relief at seeing how fast Jim was. Mech dragons were badass.

When the missiles collided with their targets, they distorted gravity around them, creating a gravitational field that suspended the nearby vrosks and trolls.

Timber and Gill leaped into the air. Timber stretched out his claws, so when he landed, they dug into the earth. A seismic blast went through the ground, knocking the vrosks off their feet.

Brath took a less measured approach to attack. He let Furi do whatever the hell he wanted, and that was to set every living troll on fire. Furi flew over the battle, firing fireball after fireball, nearly turning the canyon into a firetrap.

Jollies flew past Brath and shouted, "Hey, be careful. You're going to burn us all alive too!" Then she zoomed back into the fight, flying between troll after troll, firing her dual-energy pistols and adding to the confusion of the fight.

A troll zeroed in on Brath and took his vrosk into the air. Furi and Brath didn't notice as the vrosk flew behind them. The troll leaped from his vrosk and landed on Furi's back, then pulled out his spear and ran toward Brath.

Brath turned at the last minute, barely evading the head of the spear. He pulled out his family's knife and slammed it into the troll's foot, then tapped Furi on the back of the neck.

Furi turned his head, saw the troll, and snapped it in half with his jaws.

Below, Alex and Chine were circling the balrog, who was still cracking his whip. Around them, the battle continued. It was unclear if Boundless was going to get out of this alive. Alex didn't care, though. They were creating a distraction that would allow the minerals to arrive at their destination.

Chine's claws glowed again, and he fired another concussive blast. This time the balrog was ready for it, though. The balrog cracked its whip, breaking through the blast as it advanced. It spread its wings and flew toward Chine and slammed into the dragon. They rolled over each other, sending Alex flying through the air.

She landed on her feet as her dragon wrestled with the balrog. She was surrounded by vrosks and trolls. One of the trolls lunged for her, but she stepped to the side and brought her scythe down before drawing her energy shotgun.

As the troll's vrosk screeched and flew at Alex, she let her scythe dissolve and fired a plasma scattershot. The vrosk hit the ground and skidded across the canyon floor.

Two more of the trolls came for Alex. One of them knocked her to the ground, and she screamed in pain as the troll drove his spear through her left shoulder.

Alex still managed to aim and fire, taking off the troll's head. She scrambled to her feet, drew her scythe again, and sliced through the vrosk's legs, turning as quickly as she could and firing again before slamming her fist to her chest and erupting in a brief fury of ether fire.

Alex threw herself sideways, firing at the closest troll before rolling away and running to her dragon. Jollies flew up beside her, "Hey! Alex, if you can take care of the balrog, I have something that should clear up the rest of the trolls. But you'll need to get clear, okay?"

Alex flashed Jollies a thumbs-up and concentrated on getting back onto Chine, whose back was facing her. This was her best chance. She flung herself into the air, stretching her anchor toward Chine. The anchor connected, and Alex's feet stuck to Chine's back, even though he was on his hind legs.

The balrog had its claws around Chine's neck and was trying to sever the dragon's jugular. Alex tapped Chine's head, hoping he was still reading her mind. Then she ran up the length of his neck, down his head, and sailed through the air, her scythe drawn, and brought her blade down in the middle of the balrog's flaming skull.

It screamed in pain and backed away from the dragon, who took the opening and knocked it to the ground. Chine bit down hard on the monster's neck and tore it open, then shot an inferno of ether fire into the wound, severing the balrog's head from its neck.

Alex scampered back up Chine and pointed in the direction the mech riders had gone. "All right, everyone, move *now*! Leave the rest for Jollies!" Alex shouted.

Brath's bemused voice came through the comm. "Wait, for *Jollies*?"

"You heard what I said! Now, *move, move, move!*"

Team Boundless and Alborn's riders turned and sped toward the mechs.

Once Jollies was certain her friends were clear, she clenched her fists, and her dragon anchor glowed. Both her and Amber's bodies began to vibrate. The vibrations were so intense, they were creating multiple images of Jollies and Amber. Then the images became solid.

The canyon was filled with hundreds of Jollies and Ambers, each of them crackling energy. They all attacked, hundreds of bodies firing lightning at anything that moved.

Smoke billowed from the canyon, and there was a massive boom, then thunder and a flash of lightning. Alex looked over her shoulder to see what was happening, but there was too much smoke for her to tell.

Then the pixie and her dragon flew out of the smoke. Jollies was giggling and scratching the back of Amber's neck. "All done," she said. "If they're still alive, they won't be coming for us anytime soon. I can promise you that."

Alex air-high-fived Jollies. "Didn't know you two were packing so much power," she said, laughing.

"Big things come in small packages!"

The dragonriders sped through the canyon, leaving behind the screams and cries of the trolls and vrosks. They had a delivery to protect.

CHAPTER NINE

Alex and the rest of the dragonriders arrived at the rendezvous near sunset. She wasn't sure how long they had been riding since they had all been busy recounting the battle to each other. Alborn was frankly impressed by Alex and the rest of Boundless.

After the battle, Alborn had received a message from the mech riders, detailing that they had arrived at the processing facility in one piece. They hadn't come across any more of the Dark One's forces on the way.

Alex's gamble had paid off.

While they had been traveling to the rendezvous, Alborn had asked Alex to fly beside him so they could talk. "I'm sorry for back there," the elf apologized. "I wasn't expecting you to be nearly as capable as you were."

Alex shrugged it off and smiled sincerely. "I can see where you were coming from," she admitted. "I don't know if I would have been too keen on trusting a rookie."

"You don't handle yourself like a rookie. That was some expert commanding I saw going on back there. Not a lot of people can get that much teamwork from a team on their first mission, let alone someone who hasn't gone through the Nest's training program. Like I said, impressive."

Alborn and Alex talked more as they made their way to the facility. Alborn explained that leadership wasn't something he had ever wanted, nor was it something he felt suited for. But his family had always been military, thus he was military. He said he wished he could have been a farmer instead.

Alex listened intently as Alborn spoke. She hadn't thought about how the war had affected people who hadn't wanted to pick up a sword to begin with. It was impressive that there were people like Alborn who had answered the call of duty, regardless of their own desires.

Once Alborn was finished, Alex returned to Team Boundless, listening to Brath and Jollies talking to each other. Brath was amazed by the last attack Jollies had performed and was trying to get the pixie to tell him how she had done it.

Jollies playfully refused, trying for as many compliments as she could get. That was when Brath admitted he had been having problems with Furi. Turned out, the gnome's and the dragon's personalities were too similar, both brash and angry. It made it hard to manage together.

Gill cut into Jollies' and Brath's conversation. "That's why I keep saying you need to start meditating with me," the drow said. "It would help you calm down. Give you some inner stability."

Brath sighed and tried to ignore Gill, but he just reiterated his point, not taking no for an answer. "I'm sorry!" Brath finally exploded. "It's just so *boring*. Who wants to sit in a forest for an hour with their eyes closed, concentrating on their breathing? I'm surprised you don't go crazy."

"Calm is something a warrior must embrace. It allows

one to look at the battlefield coolly rather than being overwhelmed. Take Alex, for instance."

Alex threw up her hands, trying to keep the conversation from turning to her. "Whoa, hold on there," she interjected. "Don't bring me into this."

Gill gave Alex a quizzical look. "Why not? You were the definition of calmness today," the drow said. "We were clearly outnumbered and didn't have the support of our comrades, yet you took charge and led us to victory."

Alex blushed as she tried to find words. "Okay, for one, I didn't lead us to victory. We were all there, and we all did our part. Secondly, I was not calm. I was freaking out the entire time. Honestly, I'm surprised we're still alive."

"Exactly my point. Inwardly, you might have been tumultuous, but outwardly, you were in control."

Jim shifted on his mech's back and laughed. "Yeah, that's how Alex always was in VR," he added. "She never seemed stressed about any of the crazy stunts she was pulling. Made them look easy. Like today, when she went for the balrog's head? I would never have had the guts to do that."

Alex remained quiet, embarrassed by their praise. Chine's voice cut into her head. *Your friends respect you a lot, and so do the other dragons. It's admirable, and you've earned it.*

Alex scratched the back of Chine's head behind his ears. *You have too. You were amazing out there.*

We *were amazing.*

When the dragonriders landed at the mineral processing plant, they were greeted by the mech riders who'd transported the materials and Commander Pinelt, the overseer of the facility. Pinelt brought them inside and led them to the dining hall, where they could have a meal.

The mech riders were extremely grateful for the support Boundless and Alborn had provided. They said they would mention it in their reports.

The dining hall wasn't much different from the one at the Nest, although not nearly as magical. The dragonriders helped themselves to food from the buffet area and took their seats, ravenously eating in silence.

During the meal, Alex checked her messages to see what their next step was going to be. Their mission outline hadn't included information on what to do once they had finished transporting the minerals. "Are we just supposed to wait here until someone gets in touch with us?" she asked Gill.

Gill put down his fork and pushed his plate away. "I'm not certain," he admitted. "Probably something we should have figured out ahead of time."

Alborn and the rest of his squad had left the dining hall some time ago. Alex rose from her chair and brushed her hair back from her face. "I'm going to go check with Alborn," she told the team. "He probably has a better idea of what should happen next. I'll catch up with you guys in a bit."

Alex left the dining hall and wandered through the facility. She didn't have the slightest clue where she was going but figured it couldn't be any harder than finding her way in the Wasp's Nest, and that was when she had mostly been blind.

As Alex walked around, she saw the different areas of the facility. It seemed to be more of a processing plant than a military base. There were glass walls everywhere, which allowed her to watch the weapon-making process. Giant machines were pounding the minerals.

Elvish mages in white coats walked between the machines, checking the integrity of the minerals.

Another section was an active firing range where dwarves tested energy weapons, firing at moving targets of trolls, giants, and griffons.

Alex walked past a mage who was dressed in white and carried a clipboard. "Excuse me," Alex called. "I'm lost. You think you could help me?"

The mage looked up from his clipboard, not trying to mask his annoyance. "What are you looking for?" he snapped.

"I'm trying to find Alborn. I'm with the team of dragonriders that came with him. Team Boundless."

The annoyance left the mage's face, replaced by an eager smile. "Oh, you must be Alex Bound," he gushed. "We've been hearing a lot about your team since you got in. Great work. Uh, I believe Alborn is debriefing with the commander in the War Room. Go straight and then left at the end of the hall."

"Thanks," Alex said as she took off. When she got to the end of the corridor, she turned left and walked into the War Room.

The War Room was a cluttered mess of computer terminals and holographic projections. There hardly seemed to be any room to stand in what amounted to a cramped office. Alborn and Pinelt were standing over a holographic map.

Pinelt pointed to a spot on the map and said, "This is where the skirmish is taking place. We don't know when it broke out, but we've been trying to get ears on it for about three hours."

Alborn twirled his spindly mustache as he thought. "Have you been in contact with Roy or Toppinir?"

"We lost contact with them at the same time as everyone else. We received a distress call from Roy stating the Dark One was launching a massive attack, but he didn't give any more details. He did say he and Toppinir were going to try to stop him."

Alborn looked for a place to sit down, finally settling on a stack of boxes. "Are you saying those two went out there alone without any backup?"

"Something to that effect."

Alex cleared her throat as she stepped into the room. "Uh, we could give him backup."

Alborn jumped at the sound of Alex's voice, while Pinelt let his eyes coolly fall on the girl. "I apologize. Were you informed about this debriefing?"

Alex suddenly felt very small. She remembered she was probably still just a kid in the eyes of these two. "No," she said quietly. "I was looking for you two to see what you wanted Boundless to do since we finished our mission."

Pinelt shut down the holographic map. "Just relax. You all had a grueling first mission. Wouldn't want you to burn yourselves out."

"But you said Roy and Toppinir don't have any backup. We could provide it. You saw how well we—"

"Handled a few enemies. True, you performed wonderfully, but you're all still rookies, and this isn't a mission for rookies. Besides, Roy and Toppinir are our best riders. They can take care of themselves."

Alex walked farther into the room, then stood up straight and squared her shoulders. "Excuse me, sir. Uh, sir, that's right? Sir, if Roy and Toppinir are your best riders, don't you think it would make sense to protect them? They're valuable assets."

Pinelt rubbed the bridge of his nose. "Do not wear your welcome thin, Ms. Bound. I will not be given orders by a child."

Alborn rested his hand on Pinelt's shoulder. "If I may—"

Pinelt shot Alborn a glance of pure malice. "What is it, *Alborn*?" he hissed.

"Alex showed incredible leadership skills earlier, and her team acted with unmatched heroism, teamwork, and skill. If we are looking—"

"We are not looking. Conversation over."

Pinelt turned his furious gaze on Alex. "I advise you and your team to head to the barracks and get some rest. There might be another delivery mission for you. Dismissed."

Alex just stood there, quaking as she tried to keep from exploding. "Sure," she finally muttered. "Whatever you say."

CHAPTER TEN

Alex stormed back to the dining hall, Pinelt's words ringing in her ears. *Kids? Kids who pulled their butts out of the frying pan,* she thought. Telling her to go get some sleep like a child being sent to bed was the icing on the cake of humiliation.

When Alex walked into the dining hall, she saw her team sitting there talking quietly. No one at that table was "just a kid." They were all dragonriders, and they were here to fight the Dark One and do their parts in the war.

Alex wasn't ready to face Boundless and tell them that despite their hard work, they had been benched so the "veterans" could take care of things. Instead, Alex wandered around the facility, looking for the barracks so she could have some time alone.

Once Alex stumbled upon the barracks, she found an empty bed and sat on the bottom bunk. She opened her HUD, hoping for an update on the state of their mission. Instead, she found a message from her parents.

Alex opened it and laid back on the bed.

Her parents were beaming at her, her father tapping the

camera lens he was recording on. "Hey, is this thing on? Alex, can you hear me?"

Liza shook her head as she pointed to the camera. "George, she can't answer us. This isn't a video call, it's a video message."

"Oh, right. Well, anyway, Alex, we just wanted to say hi. We got your last message, and we're really proud of you and how you're handling yourself."

Liza pushed George out of the way so she was front and center. "That's right, sweetie! Handling bullies isn't easy, but we know you'll figure out a way to deal with it and come out better for it all. We've always been proud of your ability to stand up for yourself."

George rested his hand on Liza's shoulder. "That's right. We know you don't take guff from anyone, and I couldn't be prouder of my daughter. All right, we're signing off. Stay alive!"

Liza shot a disapproving glance at George, shouting, "George, that's not even close to funny!"

George chuckled as he reached to turn off the video. "Alex will probably think it is," he said, laughing.

The video went blank, leaving Alex alone with her thoughts. It didn't feel like she was standing up for herself right now. It felt even worse knowing that two people might be in serious danger because she was going to obey orders that made no sense.

Alex knew she should have stayed in bed, but she got up and made her way to the field outside where the dragons were being kept. She thought talking to Chine might help her clear her head.

Chine was sitting in the corner of the field, away from the other dragons. Alex waved as she approached him. *Hey!*

He raised his head and puffed out a little smoke. *Something on your mind, Dustling?*

You already know what's on my mind, don't you?

Chine's wings stretched out as he sat up. *True, but it's always better to hear it from you.*

Alex sat down across from Chine and folded her arms. She felt like a pouting child, but she didn't care. *I think the commander is full of crap. He knows he needs help, but he's too proud to admit it. And we* could *help. I know we could.*

Have you thought maybe he's looking out for your safety?

The thought hadn't crossed Alex's mind. She had assumed his decision was based on a lack of faith in her abilities. *No, not really.*

Nevertheless, he was extremely dismissive. So, what are you going to do about it?

Alex leaned back and looked up at Chine's intense black eyes. *What do you mean?*

I believe this is a question of wills, Dustling. There is the commander's will, and there is your will. Which do you believe is stronger?

Alex stormed into the dining hall. The members of Team Boundless jumped when they heard the hall's door slam. "All right. We're grounded. Literally. The commander doesn't want us going anywhere."

Brath looked up from his food. It was his third plate. "Is there somewhere to go?"

Alex sat down and nodded. "There's a battle going on. Roy and Toppinir are all alone and outnumbered. No one has heard from them in three hours. I volunteered our team to help, but the commander said we needed to stay put."

Jim watched Alex closely as he spoke. "You don't think we should?"

Alex played with one of the spoons on the table. "He

doesn't think we're qualified, or he's afraid we could get hurt. I'm not going to ask you guys to disobey a direct order or put yourself in danger because of what I think."

Gill, who was sitting on the table, his legs crossed, opened one of his eyes. "And what exactly do you think?" he asked.

"I think we should help Roy and Toppinir. I think we can handle it. I don't think we should be treated like children if we're going to fight in this war."

Jollies landed on Alex's shoulder and walked to Alex's ear. "We're going to get in a lot of trouble for this, aren't we?"

Alex smiled mischievously—the same smile that always graced her face when she was thinking about doing something reckless. "The way I figure it, we can't get in trouble if we save Roy and Toppinir, and we can't get in trouble if we're dead."

Team Boundless sat in silence for a few moments, weighing the gravity of Alex's words. Finally, Brath asked, "When are we leaving?"

Alex brought up her HUD one last time to see if they had received any updates. There were none. "Now. Let's go save Roy and Toppinir."

Alex Bound won't let the Heroes of Middang3ard die. But what can a brand-new recruit really do to save them? When it comes to Alex Bound ... a lot! Find out what in Sacrifice!

Dragons. Massive reptilian creatures with interlocking scales whose breath can burn a person to cinders within seconds. The beating of their wings bends trees at the trunk, and at full spread, they stretch a field's length. Then there are the claws—curved knives at the end of each toe that can tear flesh from the bone in one quick, leisurely swipe.

But this is just the European dragon.

There are many dragons out there in the mythos, and they're all different from one another. You've likely heard of the Chinese dragon, too—a snake-like, four-legged creature with a large head similar to a boar's. These are often paraded during festivals, but there are many other kinds of dragon in Chinese lore. Lake dragons, winged dragons, dragons that guard the underworld from thieves, two-headed dragons, shapeshifting dragons and some are even legless (not drunk, but lacking legs - although, maybe they are drunk too - who knows?)

The there are Indian dragons, Japanese dragons, Korean dragons, Slavic and Turkish and Albanian dragons… and they're not all the same thing. They have similarities, for sure, but there are enough differences there to keep things interesting. So I give you: The Diverse World of Dragons *fanfare*.

Nāga

A Nāga is an Indian dragon that often appears as a huge king cobra. They are violent and aggressive creatures that possess great muscular strength, and like the king cobra, their fangs are capable of delivering fatal venom into the bloodstream of anything that gets in their path.

Despite these characteristics, Nāgas are not all bad. Some act on the side of good, and a fair number are pretty neutral. In Hinduism, Nāgas are in fact nature spirits that guard bodies of water and can even bless the lands surrounding them. Of course, if you get on a Nāga's bad side, you can expect drought or floods - but keep it happy, and you'll get a damn fine harvest.

Unlike most European dragons, the Nāga can take a human form, and they make curious individuals. In this state they are not aggressive, but can quickly become so if angered or mistreated. In the Buddhist faith, Nāgas often have more than one head, which makes the dragon significantly more dangerous.

Japanese Dragon - Ryū

These tend to be good guys - Japanese dragons are heavily influenced by the Chinese and Indian dragons. So it's unsurprising to hear that the Japanese dragon - much like the Buddhist reading of Nāga - is associated with rain, bodies of freshwater, and the sea. There are further similarities between the two, and the Japanese borrow heavily from Indian folklore - such as the history of the underwater kingdom in which the Nāga kings live.

Ryū are snake-like in appearance and don't often have wings. They have short, clawed feet and generally are physically very similar to the Chinese Long, but usually have three claws instead of the Chinese four/five. Like many characters in folklore, the Japanese dragons are often quest-givers and can easily manipulate the texture of the world around them - perform a deed for a local dragon, and your wish to become emperor might just come true...

Bukunawa

Another moon-swallowing creature, the Bukunawa is a Philippine dragon that threatens to swallow the moon forever. However, the creature is often scared away from total digestion by loud noise or music - and in these circumstances is forced to regurgitate the moon and return home, which is deep under the sea. We know these incidents as eclipses.

The Filipinos believe there are seven moons, not one, and that these moons were created by Bathala to keep the sky light at night. But every time Bathala let a moon rise into the sky, the Bukanawa would launch itself from the water and eat it whole. Bathala wasn't impressed, but there wasn't a whole lot he could do about it, either. He instructed the island's residents to gather outside with cookware and make as much noise as possible so as to confuse and scare the dragon away.

There is a short tale that further details the history of the Bukunawa. Apparently the deep-sea dwelling creature had a sister who was a sea turtle. She would lay her eggs on the shore, but every time she did so, she would bring waves with her which would not settle back to their normal levels after she had left. So they killed the turtle, and the Bukunawa didn't like this at all. Its desire to eat the moon stemmed from this incident.

Lindworm

Away from the East we have the European dragons, which are quite different (though equally as fierce). The lindworm is one such example - a serpent creature with no wings, two claws, and an alarmingly strong jaw. You might remember the post on apocalypses - if so, then you'll remember the Norse concept of the end of the world, and how a creature known as Jörmungandr arrives on the land from the sea. Well, this foul demon is a lindworm. Perhaps the most famous lindworm of them all.

The lindworm's physical appearance can vary, however. There are lindworms with four legs or none. There are those privileged enough to have wings. However, most lindworms are snakey, slithery creatures with only two claws with which they pull themselves around.

The stories surrounding the lindworm are various - in many they occupy negative space, and are truly demonic and foul creatures. Its poisonous bite allows it to kill quickly, and so it has no reason to fear us humans. In Norse mythology, the lindworms gnaw at the very bottom of the roots of Yggdrasil, and you can see the influence of the Norse in many tales, in which the lindworms rise from below the Earth.

Wyvern

I can imagine the wyvern is familiar to many of us. We know the wyvern as a two-legged dragon with all the features typical of such a creature. There are, however, also underwater wyverns, who do not have the traditional tail, but a fin instead. Their similarities to dragons makes is difficult to tell them apart. Many a dragon has been called a wyvern by an ignorant writer, and that writer has often been turned to a charred corpse only seconds later...

Wyverns are often considered to be 'lesser' dragons. Many wyverns are incapable of breathing fire, and they tend to be smaller than the larger dragon. The wyvern is similar to the lindworm in that they operate largely with poison - though the wyvern has poisonous breath rather than a poison bite. Like the lindworm, there are no redeeming characteristics to a wyvern - they're unpleasant, foul creatures akin to demons.

Slavic Dragons - Zmey Gorynych & Zmaj

Slavic dragons have much in common with their European counterparts, except they often have more than one head and some can even regenerate limbs. The two names above are specific dragon types - the first, Zmey Gorynych, is a creature particular to Ukrainian and Russian mythology, and the second is a creature of South Slavic origin which is said to be very wise, have incredible strength, and possesses magical abilities.

Zmey Gorynych is a more traditional dragon. It has four legs, though only walks on the rear two, and does all the traditional dragon things - spits fire, munches flesh, throws people around... the number of heads isn't detailed, but paintings show the Zmey Gorynych owning three heads or more.

The Zmaj is altogether more interesting. Sure it has strength and knowledge and magical abilities, but it's also said to possess great wealth and a lustful desire for women. It can reproduce with human woman, and it lurks in the neutral zone of good vs bad. It's not the most benevolent of creatures, but neither is it the darkest evil. Like other dragons it can breathe fire, but unlike other dragons, it's often highly respected - which makes it sound like an upstanding member of the local community.

However, and most intriguingly, many national heroes have been said to be dragons. One such character was the Bosniak general Husein-*kapetan* Gradaščević who fought the Ottomans for Greater Bosnian independence. His success led to him being named 'The Dragon of Bosnia.' So dragons *do* walk among us.

They also have the Aždaja, which like the Zmey Gorynych has many heads but is a creature of absolute pure evil. It lives deep in caves and dark areas and tends to guard specific locations. It's basically a monster to slay in fairytales, which is rather unfortunate. It's not really a dragon either - more of an evil creature - but it and the zmaj get confused frequently.

There are many other types of dragon existing in the world today. Chuvash dragons, Romanian dragons, Asturian dragons... maybe we will document more in later articles!

AUTHOR NOTES MICHAEL ANDERLE

FEBRUARY 14, 2020

Thank you for reading *The Dragon Approved* stories!

Do you know about our podcast to tell you what's happening with our authors, other authors, and our releases? *No?*

Check out *Behind the Fiction* right here: (Podcast: https:// lmbpn.com/category/behind-the-fiction/).

Thank you for reading our stories and encouraging all of our authors with your kind words, wonderful reviews, and passing the news along to other readers. Believe me, sometimes just hearing fans stories about where / how / when these characters or ideas touched you makes our whole day bright and wonderful!

If you like the artwork, the artist is Jake Caleb, at JCaleb-Design.com – check out his other amazing art! Http://jcalebdesign.com

Diary, February 9ᵗʰ – 15ᵗʰ

So, it's Monday the 10ᵗʰ at the moment, and I'm already up to a few shenanigans that are cool.

At least, *in my opinion.*

A few weeks ago, we did a model shoot for one of our series. During that shoot, we took some special headshots of the model to allow us to see if we could map a real face to a 3D head. Now, that doesn't seem like anything special.

Except, we are a publishing company (trying to become an entertainment company.)

We type—a lot—and edit and publish and all sorts of things related to putting out books. Having said all that, we have been working towards 3D bodies / heads / video clips for three (3) years, and recently, Reallusion (https://www. reallusion.com) has released a way for us to use our modeling images / cover shoots for a bit more.

Take a moment (or twenty) to see the product Reallusion has released (link above) to map a face to a 3D model. I think you could have fun with it. Imagine taking a picture of your grandparent, or mom, or friend and placing them in a short animated video.

Can you *IMAGINE* the mischief you could get into? It would be *FANTASTIC!*

Now that you have the power, don't do anything evil. (I can't say "don't do anything I wouldn't do" since we all know I'm an author. *I'll absolutely do something you shouldn't do and laugh maniacally as I do it.*)

Even if you don't have the time right now, use your phone to capture the images of your friend/loved one/person you hate ranting about a subject. You will be able to use the voice to match the lips of the 3D character in the future. You just need the photos and audio at the moment. Use them when you get time.

Or, someone on Fiverr (www.Fiverr.com) will eventually offer it as a service for $50.00, I believe.

Consider it the not-very-fake deepfake (https://en. wikipedia.org/wiki/Deepfake)—the cheap version.

I'm so happy to be back in Vegas!

I'm back from the #Superstars Writing Seminar in Colorado Springs, Colorado. The people were fantastic, the relationships I formed spectacular.

The lack of oxygen was suffocating. (PUN, PUN! Wait, is that a pun?)

(*Editor's note: No.*)

(Author's Reply: *Damn.*)

It might surprise you to know that Las Vegas is about a half-mile above sea level. So, while I came down from on high, Vegas isn't exactly brimming with oxygen. This might also explain why some casinos (rumored?) pump oxygen into the casino area itself to keep people awake.

I think I might go visit the Aria to work. Maybe I'll be pumped full of oxygen.

Dammit, I need a nap, and it's only 10:30am in the morning. This jetlag is STILL kicking me in the ass.

Do enjoy your week. I'm going to go pretend to be an old man who needs his late-morning nap.

Ad Aeternitatem,

Michael

P.S. – It is Thursday the 13th (Yes, I did buy my wife something for tomorrow—I'm an author who is *not* suicidal. The purchase includes candy, not a hairdryer or washing machine, because I don't want my intelligent wife to focus on devious shit for my future. Plus, I'm going to take her to see the movie *Knives Out*. I don't want her to consider it research.)

P.S.S. – It's Friday the 14th, I've been a good husband and have not done anything to upset the excellent movie setup for tonight. T minus 3 hours, 21 minutes to not F@#%@ up. I did not make it to Friday. I gave her her gift (of the candy and plaque) about 10 minutes before midnight.

I suck at holding onto gifts.

OTHER BOOKS BY THE AUTHORS

Other Middang3ard Books

Never Split The Party (01)
Late To the Party (02)
It's My Party (03)
Blue Hell And Alien Fire (04)

Death Of An Author: A Middang3ard Novella

Other Books by Ramy Vance

Mortality Bites Series
Keep Evolving Series
Fatebound Series
Welcome to the Dragon Show Series

Other Books by Michael Anderle

For a complete list of books by Michael Anderle, please visit:

CONNECT WITH THE AUTHORS

Connect with Ramy

Join Ramy's Newsletter

Join Ramy's FB Group: House of the GoneGod Damned!

Connect with Michael Anderle and sign up for his email list here:

Website: http://lmbpn.com

Email List: http://lmbpn.com/email/

Facebook:
www.facebook.com/TheKurtherianGambitBooks